First ghosTTruth Paperback

ISBN: 978-1-0691016-2-4
Design © 2024 Mike Sauve

Cover - Andrew Brenza
Editors - Mike Sauve
Managing Director - Mike Sauve

A Book by ghosTTruth
ghosTTruth.ca
391 Rhodes Ave, Toronto, ON
M4L 3A6
An Imprint of Montag Press

MONTAG

ghosttruth

The Ghosthunter

By D.F. Lewis

W/ an Afterword
by David Mathew

THE REAL MUCKY

The first time I encountered the Gruesome Guestroom was during my geeky, nerdy project in collecting Mansions Without Roofs. Not that I ever was exactly a nerd, nor a geek, not even an anorak. I think many – especially my parents – considered me an eccentric collector of things, something that kept me off the streets, out of mischief, along the straight and narrow, and, oh, by the way, you may already have noticed that I collect hackneyed words, outworn sayings, trite expressions and other clichés. Not that you could call 'Mansions Without Roofs' a common expression; indeed, it sounds well used, a title of a book, or poem, or whatever, but as far as I have checked, it is uniquely used here. It also sounds like an expression that has been passed from generation to generation as a meaningful symbol of a state of existence that never really has existed at all. The term 'Gruesome Guestroom' is equally rare, even though a ghost story would die for it as a title. As I thought when I first encountered one such room in a Mansion that had lost its roof. Can a room without a ceiling, and open to the sky be haunted? With difficulty, I would say. There is a sense of claustrophobia in seeing ghosts, I suggest. Closed in spaces. From where you can't escape. Where the ghost – despite its tenuous existence – is trapped, too, making it pent up and thus more frightening. This Mansion was in deepest Essex and it once had stayover guests interested in hauntings and connected occult matters, a building that had now seen better days. Full of guest rooms, all of which rooms on the top floor were open to the sky. I thought this was a fine example of a mansion without a roof to tick off on my bucket list as having been visited by me.

Or as the saying goes, it was the real McCoy. Few people know that the real McCoy expression was actually coined in Glasgow as the real Mackay, but the Americans changed it to the real McCoy. Of course, I was trespassing when I visited it, as it was a dangerous building the ownership of which had been debated in courts longer than the Jarndyce & Jarndyce case. But as with The Haunted and the Haunters by Bulwer-Lytton, I loved such ghostly literature. Nothing could stand in my way. It was fenced off with the appropriate warning signs, specially the one announcing 'Danger of Death'.

I imagined falling through the lower stories once I reached the top guest rooms. But I managed to negotiate all the obstacles in my way, and to cut a long story short, ha, there I go again… I reached what I eventually called the top story, and then the Gruesome Guestroom, exactly as Midnight might have struck. Even without my torch, I could have told the time by my luminous wristwatch, as there were no working clocks. Just an eerie silence. As dead as the grave. As silent as the tomb. As unspoken as verse from the hearse. And hovering at eye-level I made out the real McCoy, something or other that gave the guest room its full name. The story halted me in my tracks. Shaken to my roots. Left me mindless, if not bodiless to boot. No skin left in the game, just the spooky bleakness that a poor bloke like me could no longer have brain to house. Death for death, breath for breath, the headless mansion gulped and shuddered. With no roof to keep it in, thus scared out of its own very skin. And mine.

MANSIONS WITHOUT ROOFS

The ghost hunter first visited this ancient set of mansions in the early part of the 1950s. Usually, one envisages a haunted mansion to be a solitary large building of some stateliness in the countryside, surrounded by woods and hills. Here, though, in the quieter quarters of a city centre were a row of such mansions with a mere narrow alley way between each one at ground level. So, not a terrace as such, but they were evidently conjoined at the upper floors. But like many terraces of smaller working-class houses, two-up-two-downs or back-to-backs as they were once called in the early twentieth century, they had attics that ran the length of their extent without interruption by any physical partition.

So, here, the ghost hunter, once clambering up to these attics, found a huge length of raftered space with uncertain flooring stretching from mansion to mansion, dark and and full of cobwebs. He held his torch steady to see what was what.

Downstairs, the living quarters were still in good shape, and in a few of the mansions their ancient families still held sway, some squatting in chairs staring through the grimy windows they could not be bothered to clean. They had allowed the ghost hunter into their domains with grudging nods. They has seen many such visits before from earlier ghost hunters to whom they charged a small fee. But this ghost hunter was different. It was me.

And I took one of the surly denizens with me upon this first torchlit visit to the now notorious corridor of attics, spanning several histories below us, each mansion having its own dynastic family. They used this area directly under the conjoined roofs as storage space. Many dark shapes of student trunks and suitcases and dolls houses and broken rocking-horses and stopped clocks provided sinister silhouettes as far as the eye could see. Many narrow gaps in the conjoined roofs supplemented my torch but I could see that, despite such gaps, there was not one sign of seepage from weather, because the gaps of light were opportunely angled to resist any fluid's passage.

That night, having returned home, I dreamt of those attics. They no longer had roofs at all, but the heavens still failed to penetrate its inclement weather within. It was as if there was an invisible skin of light stretched between the rafters that protected the storage space. A mere dream but a clue to the ghost I sought, I thought, when I awoke.

I soon forgot the dream and left for my second visit to the mansions. I sought out the same denizen who had accompanied me into the top storeys the day before. He had changed somewhat from how I remembered him, and this time he insisted on bringing his wife with us as we made a second exploration.

He told me she had once seen the ghost up there, and, despite her own natural fears of the unknown, she trusted in the ghost being a good ghost, as most ghosts seemed to me always to be, should I ever find one. She would point the ghost out to me. She knew how to sense it, to recognise it. I suddenly remembered again my dream and told them both about it. The man shrugged, but his wife smiled. As if she knew something we both didn't.

There was a child involved in their marriage who had to be cared for by another denizen of the mansion, and once that was arranged, the three of us set off, clambering through the lower partitioned attics towards the upper corridor of attics. Strangely, I had not noticed the lower attics yesterday, but I was never an infallible witness, and I shrugged my shoulders at this hole in my memory.

I invite you, nevertheless, to follow my hunting as far as I was able to reach that day. We managed to walk, in a stooped way, the whole length of the mansions. Listening to what was going on below in each of them, the sound of dynastic families passing through levels of time towards this era of chaos that seemed gradually to be affecting the whole world. The odd Singer sewing machine being treadled. Children's voices. And a gramophone needle's scratching. Prior to music sounding out.

Some of the gaps in the roof were now more like holes. And the bric à brac stored up there seemed to have skeletal outlines rather than yesterday's unbroken shapes back to back. One rocking horse was now a cage. One of us opened it. But it still rocked with the rhythm of a clock, as the heavens above shone through the holes with what I imagined the Holy Ghost to be. The rest was forgotten. But it was not a dream this time.

'A GHOST STORY'

The figure entered the hallway with a pure white head – the term 'head' including the whole face where the hair, mouth, nose and ears should have been, but on one side was a single large vertically eye-shaped hole to let any light through. The outline of the face itself was moon-wide upon a black neck that led to a body dressed in what appeared to be an armless black gown in the otherwise dim space in which I stood watching it.

It was a household that eked out its electricity supply with proud stubbornness, so everywhere in it was mainly dark, with the denizens currently sitting in the only fully lighted room in the whole mansion. They indeed called it their sitting-room.

I had not expected such an apparition, but being what I like to call a ghost hunter, indeed *the* ghost hunter, I should not have been surprised, let alone as shocked as I was. But bearing in mind that this was my very first ghost apparition to witness, any emotion could have been excused, ranging from a love of awesome things to a mild fear, then to this utter terror. From frisson to a prison of self. Shutting every sense down so as to block out what I had seen. Not even shouting out to those in the sitting-room.

Whether the ghost had vanished after my initial sight of it,

I was never to discover. All I can remember is that there was one slit in my soul that let it in like light. The next time you read some narrator's words claiming to be *the* ghost hunter in a series of forthcoming short ghost stories like this one, it will not be me.

THE GRUESOME GUESTROOM

The ghost hunter's next assignment of a haunted mystery was one he thought he had once cracked earlier, as he already had a title for it. Déjà vu was not a luxury he would countenance, so he remained determined to follow it through, whatever corners he had to turn more than once.

He knew the room in question was on the top floor of a mansion near Chelmsford, and he ordered a taxi to reach it, bearing in mind the rail strikes prevalent at the time. He hated unexpected points or signal failures, in any event. As the car wound up the long drive, he remembered he was only half invited, as it were. So he had his own story to tell once he knocked on the front door, depending on who opened it. The elderly couple who lived there with many servants did not see eye to eye, and only one of the couple had arranged this assignment for the ghost hunter.

Neither of them, as it happened, opened the door to him. It was, of course, one of the servants, so the ghost hunter was a little at a loss for words.

So, it was me who climbed the interminably winding stairs behind the footman. He knew exactly why I was there. He was obviously in cahoots with the one who had assigned me to this task, because surely, otherwise, he would have taken me in completely the wrong direction. We reached what he called the guestroom in question, and it turned out to be beyond the top storey, as it happened, being more an attic than a pukka floor.

He nodded me to open the door to this guestroom myself, with no sense of suspense. And the climax was already there before me. Nothing signalled in advance.

Attics were known to have rafters. But this one had what I can only call a flat ceiling, pure white from corner to corner, with fine cornices. Or were they covings? This was the disguised ghost of the mansion, I knew. Stretched in smooth pity or pain. As if it should not be there at all. But simply needed to be there as spectral witness.

The footman withdrew, leaving me with my own quandary. Beneath this 'ceiling', were the prone figures of an elderly couple, hands positioned in prayer, as if carved in stone for an old country church. I managed to leave quietly, retracing the route of what I now knew for certain to once have been déjà vu.

Not a gruesome guestroom after all, as there was no blood, simply peace and quiet. I took one rubbing from the brass plinth at the foot of their 'bed' as a keepsake. Not even a guestroom full stop. I simply guessed they were not guests of the elderly couple in the mansion. But the elderly couple themselves.

And, back home, he knew he was the ghost hunter, after all, now pleased with yet another tale to re-tell.

MANSIONS WITHOUT ROOMS

/had a dream once. Well, several dreams, in fact. All ghost hunters do. So, I suppose being the ghost hunter means I have more dreams than most. Within the special dream to which I am drawing attention here, I dissociated myself from the self dreaming it and became the man in it, not, as such, a ghost hunter at all, but an interested party in the side issues of such matters. He was asked to visit a few mansions in the Norfolk area of England, and coming from Clacton, he needed to travel from train via Colchester. The mansions themselves probably never existed outside of this special dream of mine.

The Clacton man was an insurance official, a claims adjuster and a property valuer combined, and of course ghosts were capable of causing insurable damage to properties as well as affecting the value of such properties. The value of a property, in this context, went up or down according to the imaginative or sensitive temperament of any purchaser of it, of course. A yearning to see ghosts as some form of mortality blocker. Or a feeling of terror at the thought of such things.

To cut a long dream short, I still feel a frisson of disquiet at what transpired in this dream to the man in it, a man who was only similar to me by living in Clacton, as I do, and, indeed, I, too, once worked in insurance many years ago as a company pensions negotiator. Actuaries, whether in the annuity or life insurance business, in those days, I recall, yearned for or were terrorised by mortality-blockers in equal measure! Still do, I guess. And, oh yes, I wrote the old story 'Digory Smalls' where a man takes a stunted dwarf into a series of interlocking attics in a mansion above the various floors containing rooms.

The mansions in the dream were set side by side in an area of Norfolk that was little known. Not a terrace of mansions as such, but certainly a row. With an allotment between each one. Tended by inhabitants of those mansions, vegetables for their own consumption.

The area had seen better days. But the crux of the matter, as the insurance official discovered, was that all the mansions contained no rooms at all! They were constituted of a whole complex of interlocking attics, interlocking even with other mansions in the very top levels by dint of some upper crooked architecture that counteracted the gaps between these mansions lower down.

The last thing I remember when cutting a longer dream short, was being carried by this man through these dusty raftered attics, full of childhood's bric à brac, towards some force of nature that counteracted nature itself. Azathoth was a name somehow imprinted on my mind, as I struggled with the hatches between each attic, using loft ladders galore in what I can only call tessellated lattices, just with the use of my stunted limbs like small flippers.

The man in this special dream eventually abandoned me up

there, you see, and a version of me is still there seeking immortality, but being blocked at every turn. I need to dream the dream again to attempt rescue of myself. Or from myself? The trains are now on strike, though.

THE THIRD BED

As ghost hunter, I had encountered many situations where the sleeping occupant of one bed next to an empty one, sensed a haunting that emanated from such a situation. So when I was requested to investigate a case where — for some reason I failed to grasp — there were three separate beds in a room, I could not resist answering such a call to duty.

Yes, it was a large room! It was in an old boarding house in a seaside town not far from Clacton. In fact, this nearby town was where I was born 75 years before, but that is beside the point.

When I was first told of the circumstances, intrigue overwhelmed me, with my being a great fan of Elizabeth Bowen's 'shadowy third' syndrome, where a couple felt an extra presence stalking them. Or even perhaps overseeing them benignly.

Quite often, a third that was in love with one or the other of the people with whom it was obsessed. Normally, a ghost but sometimes a real person. Rarely, if ever, was this 'third' a hybrid of ghost and real person, needless to say.

To reach this place, luckily I did not need a train. A bus would suffice, and if I were younger a long walk would have achieved my goal. So the bus it was. The last bus of the day. I had been unavoidably delayed, you see. I planned to book a taxi back home, after completing the assignment. But it never came to such a necessity. You can guess why.

ALONE WITH THE HORRORS

Whereas in these stories of self and non-self I am labelled the ghost hunter, such a label also entails dreamcatcher or hawler of literature, sufferer of pareidolia and apophenia, finder of found art on sea, beaches, woods and skies, and above all, when alone, someone who feels he is haunted and hunted by those he in turn haunts and hunts. The ghost haunter, too, then, you might already have guessed.

This particular tranche of plot tells of when I investigated 'The Third Bed' mystery in the very seaside town where I was born. Allowed actually to sleep in such a bed as part of some experiment in self-haunting. Staring up at the bedroom ceiling which was as evidently as white during darkness as it was during daylight. A house big enough to be called a mansion with the name Olive Villa. Otherwise, boarded up, despite the pure whiteness of its ceilings, even whiter and brighter upstairs than downstairs. I tried to drift my mind into sleep with memories of dreamcatching certain literature, such as that written by Satyamurthy, Sauve, Zelenyj, Hughes, Hirshberg, Heuler, Leyshon, Wyckoff, Miskowksi, dePackh, Pflug, Bartlett, Holmes, Crisp, Watt, Travis, Mathew, Royle, Lynch, Grant, Scofidio, Rix & Ruppert along with other Axes of Chaos and Order

But the heavy breathing of the elderly couple sleeping in

the other two beds kept me awake, with my ever listening for such breathing to cease. It was so very dark, despite the widening brightness above me.

Meanwhile, in hope or dread, he keeps one vertical eye open.

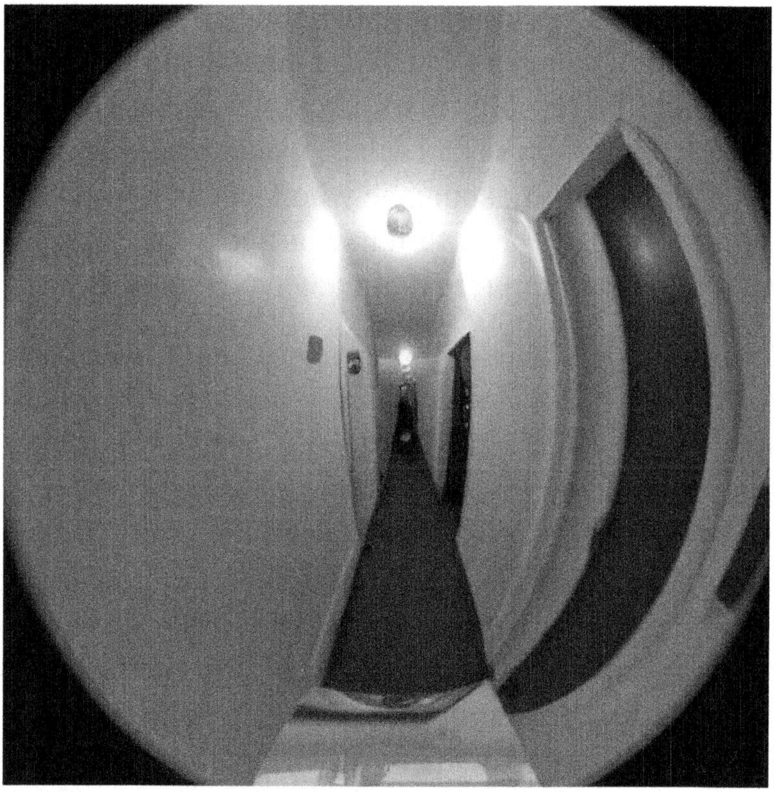

GHOST HUNTING FOR THE GHOST HUNTER

As soon as we knew that not just any ghost hunter but *the* ghost hunter had gone missing when on their latest assignment, we pulled out all the stops to find them.

Who are we, you ask? Well, the best way to describe us would be a loose organisation of other ghost hunters, most of us real people with interests in such matters, mostly level-headed citizens with a leaning towards the paranormal because we yearned admittedly for such a mortality blocker, being romantic souls with open eye-shaped apertures ready to welcome in the light of such spirituality beyond our normal lives. There were a few mad ones, too, perhaps, and even a number of shadowy thirds masquerading as real people, a tiny few among the latter being at least partially ghosts themselves.

Whoever we were in the view of third parties, we were quite different from each other in many ways, all genders and orientations and creeds, and we had one goal, to find the ghost hunter who represented us all. We hunted this ghost hunter in all the places we knew they frequented, mansions without roofs, mansions without rooms, searching even the most far-fetched attics beyond sane ceilings or storey dividers. We searched the pareidolia of skies, seas and woods, the gestalt apophenia of poetry, fiction and literature, the scurrilous avenues of AI art and for the first time we indulged in the experience of hunting real paintings for ghostly shifting of overnight changes in them. And, of course, and now with a look of importance in our faces, we hunted within the music we knew they loved: viz. Beethoven, Schubert, Mahler, Schoenberg, Glass, Nurse with Wound and the late work of the late Scott Walker.

And we eventually found what we knew somehow was the Real Mucky, a blind idiot god with flutes and drums, and frights so frightful, we screamed. Whether it was *the* ghost hunter transmigrated into the light they thought they had seen we shall never know. Most of us who were able to do so went back to our normal lives without beliefs in anything beyond such lives. Once bitten, twice shy, most of them. One of us, though, still wanders the now renewed wastes of your minds, still hunting for ghosts beyond the mirrored ceiling of gestalt, knowing someone simply has to fulfil this duty for a reason that has yet to be defined better than it was earlier defined above in this very tract that you now read, someone or something beyond pronoun's reach that sits within you as you read it.

THE POINTING GHOST

I now reach a watershed or non-sequitur, as I suddenly recall, from my childhood, a ghost that relentlessly pointed at me with its finger, for as long as I managed to stay awake when sitting on my nursery rocking-horse. But when I did sleep, I dreamt of the ghost still pointing at me. Except in the latter case, I was the ghost and the ghost was me sitting on my rocking horse. In those days, I did not know I was to become a ghost hunter, and I often wonder what that dream must have presaged — but, calling a spade a spade as the cliché goes, let's call this dream what it really was, a sheer utter nightmare of terror involving confusion about what pointed at whom or who pointed at what upon the now stiff and stifled rocking of the rocking horse. Did this nightmare actually trigger my destiny in becoming a ghost hunter, often providing a similar confusion as to whether I was to become a ghost haunter, instead? A finger continuously pointing at myself in some form of bony rigour that was far more mortifying than just a calm drifting away into a brain-softening old age, the endgame of which I once called, with relish, an 'eventernal slumber' (please Google this term) or was it the state of what has since become known in my head as 'null immortalis'? Meantime, when you arrive at a watershed in a series of telling events, it is all too easy to make the break clearer by employing a new paragraph or even a small line of asterisks to show that you are turning a page, or leap-frogging a cliffhanger. These stories, it increasingly becomes clear, are separate floors in the mansion of life, till you reach the topmost attic of all, from which vantage point of near roofless exposure, you can gather, simply by looking down, that the whole crumbling exterior of the mansion badly needs repair. And yet the dark shapes that climb the outer walls, despite such crumbling, fail to carry trowels for the necessary 'repointing' (a term you hope is understood even by any non-building workers). In fact, they seem to be wielding implements far more disturbing. You desperately yearn to be rocked asleep into an unimpeachably full 'null immortalis' before they can reach you or, failing that, you must simply yearn to be given, by an overarching power, the surprise gift of a real unicorn horn as the only known antidote to their approach. You see, death and its denizens are reputedly their own non-sequitur. Time will tell, as the cliché says.

THE MANSIONS OF THE MOON

More as a dream catcher than as a ghost hunter, although ghosts were surely involved, I took a rocking-horse ride to the dark side of the moon whereon a multitude of shapes and figures pointed at me with steady fingers from the rooftops of renovated mansions. All this, beyond the mutually disguised chaos and order of the Real Mucky that now prevailed in Earth's ruined streets and the fury of wild-fiery terrains.

Here, on Moon's obverse, therefore, resided hope of rescue for those who might follow me, despite the paranoia-inducing pointing of the mansions' denizens already here. The people remaining below on Earth would use, no doubt, their own chosen means of an erstwhile childhood's transport as and when needed to dream themselves here for real. And then for them to ignore the pointing from those on the mended rooftops already here, and to build their own mansions of fulfilled expectation.

Did I wake reluctantly from this dream's later eclipse? It is for me to know, and for you to find out.

I was simply reminded of a different childhood and a different grown-up version of me who could not believe in ghosts even when haunted by them. They teemed around me at every corner of my life, I have since discovered. They were there when I was at work and when I was at play, even during a period of parenthood amid the new toys thus involved, and even under the effects of later illness and sore urination, before visiting the elderly couple carved upon a tomb, all in pure white stone, a whiteness to match the ceiling above them.

I took such memories to the mansions on the moon whereby to fill the cracks in their walls. Yet the whiteness of my cement made the cracks look worse against the original moon rock of the walls that my cement healed. I would need to paint all over them to make the disguise fully work. All completed under the tessellated lattice of ladders to heaven or hell as formed by pointed fingers each grown into a bony elbow.

Did I wake less reluctantly this time from a second dream's eclipse? It is for me to know, and for you to find out. But you seem to have departed already towards the moon's bright white horn of bone now straightening — even as I watch it as above, so below — into a vertical eye's ellipse.

THE MANSIONS OF THE ROOM

'As above, so below', is an easy meme, for example to reconcile my interests in the believable power of synchronicity rather than in the more superstitious cause-and-effect effect of cosmic bodies and patterns upon us all. You see, even astrology becomes believable in that very light, the perceived power of the moon being a fine way to contextualise this consideration. Indeed, by the way, the word 'mansions' is an official term in the art or science of astrology as derived from the ancient form of astrology. From the Internet: 'Often called lunar mansion, a lunar station or lunar house is a segment of the ecliptic through which the Moon passes in its orbit around the Earth.' You may be interested to know that I used to follow planetary transits upon my own Natal Chart. Meantime, ghost hunters and dream catchers are creatures of 'the synchronised shards of random truth and fiction', as I hope my recent stories show, building eventually towards a gestalt that will not counteract against the ability of these stories to be separately read in a gulp, each managing to stand thus alone. Each a stone alone in the universe but susceptible to the universe's patterns.

I once had an assignment to hunt a ghost in a mansion near St Osyth and in what I guess to be the biggest children's nursery room in the whole world! A nursery used for an only child, to boot! Incidentally, I am conscious I may have given you the impression that I am an exorcist, but no, I am a freelance ghost hunter, with my own yearning to witness a real ghost as a comfort blanket or mortality-blocker, someone who is in fact often employed by my customers to establish a ghost's existence for their own similar satisfaction, but not for me to destroy or remove such a ghost. There is quite a difference.

The room in fact, I hasten to add, in hindsight, used to be a nursery but this was no longer the case, the child having long grown up and left home. However, it was preserved exactly as the erstwhile child had left it, scattered with toys, many of which were dolls houses as far as the eye could see. I counted at least a hundred of them. Or should I call them dolls mansions? They looked like mansions to me, most with liftable roofs or openable frontages, to reveal the rooms. Yet, unlike the actual real mansion housing this main once-nursery room which itself housed such 'toy' mansions, these so-called 'toy' mansions, I soon discovered, had been gutted of their rooms altogether as if to make the largest internal space possible in each one — as if to suit dolls that were gigantic when judged by the scale of the buildings themselves. So that they could stand with feet in the basements and heads against the insides of the roofs. All ceilings gutted, all partitions or rafters, too.

I suddenly stopped in my tracks of thought. Did I just say 'basements' somewhere in my report above? How possibly could a traditional 'dolls house', as these mansions effectively were, have basements? The concept was unthinkable for obvious reasons.

MISSPOKEN AND MEANT MENTIONS

There was a time when I wasn't any old ghost hunter let alone *the* ghost hunter, and I was even investigated for malingering as non-existent. I did no work at all, you see, until I heard the call, my first assignment being to establish a ghost in the ready-made ruins of St Botolph's Priory, Colchester. The council needed it to bolster the tourist trade, as nobody seemed to visit this otherwise attractive place except winos. So, disguising myself as one of those winos, I, too, sat in this shaded, hillocky precinct out of mind and time, near the streets of charity shops yet strangely also so far away from them. An ancient ruined place that needed to achieve the magnetic heft of the more renowned Norman Castle in that town, now city.

But no ghost submitted its presence to my hunting, so I resorted to dream catching it instead, hauling, in my mind, every piece of the crumbling structure into new configurations that would strip any ghost of its non-existence behind or within such items of now malleable rubble it may have hidden. The other winos stared at me, as I sat in a state of half sleep, half waking, indeed half human, half ghost, juggling with a new physics, a new path for reality, and despite having misspoken many times since that first assignment about never yet having established the existence of any ghost, let alone *the* ghost, I did that day come as close as close can be to doing so. I only mention such later failings on my part as ghost hunter so as to give the ghost more credence, distilled as it was from your disbelief now suspended.

You see, yes, you can surely see, the actual disturbing shape hanging between Priory Street and St Botolph's Church, floating without support, a configured tranche of history in this oldest recorded town, now city, the oldest in the whole of Britain. A blasphemous blend of all the history lessons that we have endured throughout our serial schooldays, a deconsecration utilising a huge sucking maw to motion its intentions. It meanfully moved with its own robotic but spiritually tenuous limbs, as well as engulfing, with its autonomous mouthings, whoever of us glimpsed its form of lies, the winos as spear-carriers included,

So, if truth were told, the ghost hunter had already fled, without even a glimpse of this so-called ghost, like Darcy fleeing from Ms Bennett in an alternate version of Pride and Prejudice. Or like the allies fleeing the aliens in a new world war. With no mentions of mansions. Just ruins. A tourist trap to die for.

As the crucial planetary transit of the day clicked into place in my brain, that brain had a brainwave. I had found a real ghost at last. The once unthinkable concept was now well and truly trapped between four walls and a roof. No escape for it now.

But I knew I was on the ground floor of the mansion, and beneath my feet I heard the sudden noises of awakening by things that would give me nightmares for the rest of my time on Earth. So, I fled into the moonlight outside the main mansion while I had a chance to do so, without waiting to seek payment from the customer for my ghost hunting services and without any desire for the mortality-blocker's comfort blanket that I once hunted. But even so, I am nevertheless beset by the nightmares I feared would have come to me had I stayed in that room!

ἀπὸ μηχανῆς θεός

I've deliberately delayed telling you about one particular assignment for me to establish a ghost, because its circumstances seem to stretch credence beyond anywhere credence is supposed to go!

But when I say one particular assignment, there were two assignments in truth, but strangely, in hindsight, connected into one. By the way, I use the word 'credence' instead of 'belief' advisedly, because it gives the necessary church ambiance, and, after all, many M.R. James stories took place in churches, perhaps without even one mention of God, only mention of the carved pews and the people who worked there, whether Rector or Vector diverted. Or do I mean Verger? Even Sexton? Those aforementioned paths of reality with which I once juggled in the grounds of St Botolph's Priory. And churches do make a welcome change from mansions, I guess.

Whatever the case, upon curating these many so-called ghost stories, I have tried delaying the telling of this one because of the personal connections? No, because it was damn frightening. It is nothing I can really convey through the words that I type here, but deep down the frights remain, and you will have to take that as read. You will never be able to feel these frights unless you had experienced them alongside me.

The first 'assignment' was the Wivenhoe church, in a township near Colchester with tea places, antiques and bookshops, the church itself with a construction on its tower that looked like a much smaller version of the old-fashioned bandstand from Colchester Castle Park. The other 'assignment' was St Andrew's Church, Coulsdon in Surrey, near Croydon, a relatively nondescript church on a suburban hill that had no connection whatsoever with the Wivenhoe church. Coulsdon, incidentally, was, and probably still is, a place nobody would visit unless they had to!

At first I thought the cases were quite separate and thus I treated them as such. Before I go much further, you will be astonished to learn that I never actually set foot in either of these churches as part of my paid ghost hunting, although I do recall many many years before attending a choral concert in the Coulsdon church. Memories are ever uncertain at my age.

It was simply the 'credence' stretching between the two sites that eventually indicated what I was up against. I've told you before I am not an exorcist, but an establisher, or opter, of ghosts so as the customer asking me to do this can exploit the hauntings for whatever purpose they have in mind. And somehow I established a flyover, half real highway, half Heavenly arch, stretching between the two churches, and spanning all the counties between. With outlandish vehicles, it seemed, negotiating its complex lanes and hard shoulders, whether driven by ghosts or not, with the thickest brown smog imaginable pouring from outsized exhausts.

Needless to say, I was never remunerated for my findings. They, whoever *they* were, blocked my findings from all records. This is the first time they have been made public. But I still have that particular over-weening ghost somewhere in all the contraptions of life that I use, even the one used to type this. Deus Ex Machina. Grating atonally like a wind band with rusted or corroded instruments.

PRECARIOUSLY PITCHED BETWEEN TRUTH AND UNTRUTH

There was a period in my life when I yearned to surrender all goals in my career of ghost hunting or, as I now prefer to call it, 'ghost establishing'. Having failed to fully establish any ghost, it seemed pointless to continue, although my reputation remained good for almost establishing a real ghost on several occasions. Perhaps, as similar to Holmes, I should recruit an assistant to bear some of the burden, before handing in my spiritual dowser!

After several auditions, a better word obviously than 'interviews' in the circumstances, I decided to do without! But the process had enlivened my interest and confidence in the activity of ghosts and hauntings. One man called Smith, for example, provided evidence of fully established ghosts that he had encountered when working for other practitioners. I took these claims with my usual cliché of a pinch of salt. Funny that, though, thinking about it in hindsight, throwing a pinch of salt over one's shoulder into the Devil's eye was a superstition unworthy of a pukka ghost hunter, but actually to take matters with a pinch of salt was to preserve sceptical caution over a claim precariously pitched between truth and untruth, a claim often already swinging toward the latter. But that was not the last time I encountered Smith. It was when the balance was due to swing the other way, like a hopefully blunt pendulum over the Real Mucky's pit I later found myself in.

As someone always ready to wield a hackneyed phrase, I now cut a long story into a short-short, by saying that the assignment that saved me from retirement as ghost hunter was a story title given to me, 'Mansions Without Roofs', picked randomly out of a tin of many prepared titles on slips of paper useable for the writer's group to which I belonged in Clacton. And I quickly scribbled out what was due to be typed, as if it were one of our customary speed-writing exercises, but retitled it 'The Real Mucky' instead of the original given title from the random tin, having by then deleted the most horrific bits I had written that genuinely scared me, still do in fact. And also to safeguard the other members of the group.

One day I shall try to remember exactly what it was I wrote and later deleted, hopefully then to block it forever by catharsis. What I originally wrote, however, must have autonomously established a ghost for real, either by a code or occult means, which was my ultimate ambition of ghost-establishment that still dogs me, indeed established such a ghost with irresistible certainty and with no hope of exorcism. Not a daemon muse as such, but an incubus that was too soft and mucky to prevent itself melting all over me.

The only way to escape such a nightmare was to make a certain promise to the Real Mucky that has haunted me ever since, a sacred promise (now fulfilled) of replacing the given title of my assigned homework in the group I had attended for well over twenty-five years. Meantime, Smith, as

I remembered him, turned out frighteningly to be an alias, the alternate truth of a monster's namesake, a key to the code I had somehow written. But that is now water under the bridge, hopefully.

I later wrote a different sanitised story for the group and gave it the title 'Mansions Without Roofs', my penance thus come full circle. Touch wood.

CRAQUELURE

The painting did not become clear till he had wiped over its surface with a specially prepared cloth, using a mild purpose-made chemical that wiped away dirt, dust and other foreign bodies without harming the paint itself. It also wiped away any illusions that what was in front of him would not be a major discovery for any art dealer to die for.

The art preserver's partner whistled under his breath, the only way to describe the sound of awe at what he saw over the art preserver's shoulder. The lady in the corner, the inherited owner of the painting, craned her neck to get a better view of it, the preserver's own blinkered enthusiasm not allowing him to think about moving to allow her to see more. He had felt the contours of the paint and its enticing craquelure under the cloth that he had gently wiped across its mentally marked out areas requiring meticulous treatment one by one. It made his fingers tingle. Never had he felt a painting like it. Indeed, actually to feel a painting tactilely is a separate experience from simply seeing it, with both processes complementing each other in a synergy with indefinable power. Most people only receive the experience of simply seeing a painting, unless they or a friend had painted it and thus allowed to touch it. I was now touching it through the tenuous skin of empathy. But rarely could most people touch a now obviously radiating masterpiece like this one by an as yet unknown artist of the art-heavy past. These were *never* experiences obtainable with AI art in any case, one reason I can feel confident that such art will never prevail over real art, however fine the former's images. But the lure remains.

Until the artist's name is established, I have left many of the other names unspoken here, the art preserver himself, his partner, the lady who owned the painting, and her besuited son who now entered the room scowling that they had started the process without him. I have also delayed describing or naming the painting's images revealed, all richly coloured, some apparently thickly applied with an ancient palette knife. Its overall impression empathically evolving under thinly cloth-insulated fingers was startling, suffice it to say at this stage.

You see, as I write this, the process is incomplete. The gestalt only to be guessed. It had soon become clear that it was a diptych with the other half hinged to the upper half but sitting below it, and much care would be needed in dislodging the embedded one, face down as it was to the back of the glassless frame. We intend to tackle this tomorrow. I say 'we' but it is mainly me who does the intricate work of ghost hunting, more difficult, I claim, than the meticulous acts of art preservation.

*

Many of my previous assignments of ghost 'pareidolia' were with various forms of music and literature and indeed previous examples of painting or other fine and found art, and there are more tales of those disciplines in my later ghost hunting accounts as sort of allusive fiction-truths, particularly the discipline (or indiscipline?) of some atonal music, and this, in fact, is something for you to look forward to when I get round to writing them up for you.

But now, the next day has indeed dawned, and I can reveal that the opening of the back of the frame was easier than anticipated as if some trap was making it easier for us to *be* trapped by it!

None of us — and you can only guess at the backstories and current interactions of us all in this story that would take a whole novel to tell! — yes, none of us could have predicted what eventually transpired, even though the lady's supercilious son had insisted that I, as professional ghost hunter, had been present at the operation. The artist's name never became clear, as I understand it, so I am forced to allow any other names to remain elusively undivulged, however otherwise alluring they may be. An act of sacred Nemonymity on my part.

Yet, I can now bruit it publicly about many of the repercussions of this second day of the art preservation, the first clue to which was that some of the images cleaned into view the previous day seemed to have slightly shifted overnight. And one figure had taken on a possible resemblance to a well-known figure in our previous government in a pose he would not have wanted witnessed, and with what Blakean company he kept.

The back of the frame indeed revealed the hinge to the

second half of what I still deemed to be a diptych, and after some more systematic cleaning area by area by the pre-server, thus making my own fingers tingle, we stood there with open mouths, reflecting similar mouths we now saw within the literally creaking craquelure, as if the paint was in pain. And we now realised there was another hinge to a 'shadowy third'! A ghostly *tripswitch* toward something I had always yearned to experience. The others, meantime, went their own ways, beyond the frame of this brief story.

ATONALIA

I think it is the common factor in all ghost hunters — well, all those worth their salt — that they enjoy the niche sound art of atonal music, whether it be Arnold Schoenberg or the old collective of musicians called Nurse With Wound, and many others such as Barraqué, Berg, Boulez, Zann and the late sessions of the late Scott Walker. Why this should be the case, I have my theories, but the reason became slightly clearer with what I have referred to before as the Case of the Third Bed.

It was where 'Oh Whistle' became 'Oh Scream One's Heart Out', beside the sea, near the second longest pleasure pier in England. It was when the ghost hunter as narrator of events effectively made the haunted extra bed full with my investigative bodily presence, instead of this bed's apparent customary emptiness, while an old married couple breathed heavily and rhythmically in apparent near unbroken sleep in the other two beds nearby. Only for them to suddenly wake and find indeed with terror that their spare bed was full. The combined 'musical' sounds heavily leaking from my several bluetooths must have scared them with more than just the hologram of a ghost that was sculpted in the air from the unexpected shape in the bed, cross-tempered with the various zany angles and the odd acoustics of their empty attic with a broken ceiling and the raging seas outside, the flutes, violins and drums within each of the seas' relentless rhythmic surges, just like another Old One's breathing.

I somehow managed to make peace with the elderly couple, a little the worse for wear from their panic at the sight of an unexpected guest and adding their own precarious mortality to the gestalt of patterns, and I was more than just happy in my heart that potential real ghosts could be created from any chance configurations of reality, as if through a sort of cosmic pareidolia. A lesson for all good ghost hunters.

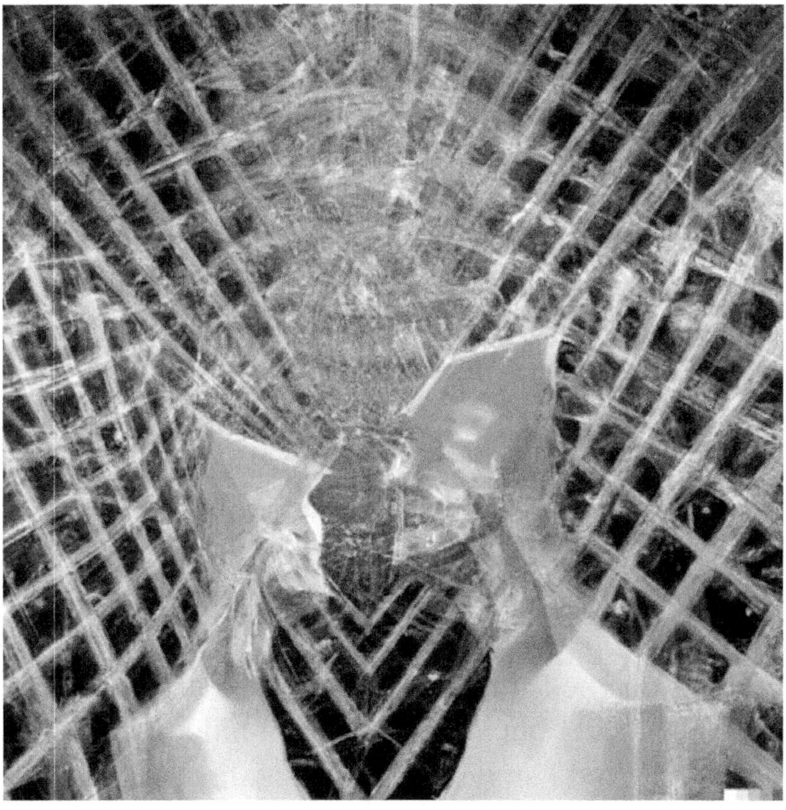

FOR THE FORMING AND ASSIMILATION OF A SMILE

The next assignment is a second example in this series that derives from either déjà vu or blatant retelling, I am not sure which. In old age memory fades. This time the ghost as pareidolia involves my favourite stamping ground, so surprising it has not cropped up in this series of fiction-truths till now. It is opportune, however, as I have recently decided that the original Real Mucky was not real at all, not even an alter ego of Azathoth, merely a ghost with a fluid excess of ectoplasm, in just the same basic way as I currently have a medicinally induced excess of sporadic sweat upon my body. Just a ghost as real or unreal as those in my favourite ghost stories by M.R. James, Oliver Onions, E.F. Benson, H. Russell Wakefield, L.P. Hartley, Edith Wharton etc. etc., even in the more complex spectral constructions of Walter de La Mare, Elizabeth Bowen, Robert Aickman and Thomas Ligotti. Yet my recent brief accounts seem to contain real ghosts, if one scries the pareidolia and apophenia of their words with an open mind, not merely to discover signs of the obvious yearned-for ghost always only almost there as a mortality-blocker but a quite different hidden ghost that is truly there! And I smile at such a tantalising thought.

*

Holland Haven is upon the Essex Edge where sea defences have recently been transformed from the old fashioned wooden groynes, those wide-toothed combs for Giants, now reborn as fishtail promontories of imported geology surrounded by deepened levels of sand, so deep that each old concrete or wooden stairway down to the sea has been buried up to the neck within swathes of newly wide-spread beachhead.

The waves find it impossible to climb these man-made heaps of gritty yellow and brown, but how long will tidal surges be outdone by these dunes let alone by the rocky two-fingered fishtails intended somehow to trick such surges away from the shore?

That trick seems to be based upon a pattern of angles by hidden geometry whereby these sea defences sweep water into confusions of direction, causing tide to neutralise tide, one in ebb, the other in flow. The quenching of thirsty energy with each swell and counterswell of mutual gulping.

The apparent Holland Haven local thereabouts smiled at me when I told him about my theories upon the mysterious nature of the fishtails and heightened sand. He was a strange man who seemed to spend his time taking photographs of these new sea defences with his battered iPhone. He had a wealth of photographs, he told me, showing the building of them from scratch. Also photos of this area before the coming of the fishtail builders. He was not interested in science or engineering, however, he told me; he was more of an artist who, by some instinctive framing, preserved the shapes and sculptures of man-made structures interacting with natural ones. An open-air Tate Gallery, he evidently hoped.

He suddenly pointed at what looked like a variegated flotsam of attic bric-a-brac bobbing gradually into view around the tip of the nearest rocky fishtail. I squinted my eyes to see at what he was now repeatedly clicking his iPhone. Floating there were what appeared to me to be framed paintings, all a bit worse for wear from being in the sea. They clunked and clicked together upon the tide, at first seeming to approach the beach where we stood, then growing more distant, each move forward immediately followed by a move back like a latter day Zeno or Sisyphus, the trend being to travel parallel with the Edge of Essex, not inward nor outward.

We walked to keep pace with them, getting nearer to an area of the coast where yellow mechanical diggers and lorries were still building the fishtails and other sea defences. We would soon be stopped in our tracks by barbed wire.

'That's the Mona Lisa,' he suddenly said, as I watched one painting, looking remarkably like that actual iconic portrait with its famous smile from the Louvre, as it bobbed out of sight behind a few randomly piled rocks.

'Surely a copy,' I said confidently with a forced smile of embarrassment to cover my retreat of fear at this madman.

'Nope,' he said coolly, 'that's the original.'

He had taken a quick iPhone snap of my face. He then took another cursory snap, this time of the rocks around which the painting had vanished upon some tidal current nobody could have explained or predicted, least of all the engineers who had allowed this current to exist from the random positioning of several fishtails and heaped-up sand.

His photos, I infer, were not direct records of observed things but more like trying to cohere the Platonic Form of Smile. Not a Cheshire Cat's smile nor even a ghost's, but a smile created by waves and suchlike as found art, in the Zeno's Paradox of our perceived time and space.

But this story about him was never to be the destination, just a way station. Images, painted or snapped alike, are human first or artificially created second; they ever ebb and flow in dilatory uncertainty. Words are waves and suchlike, too, equally confused and conflated with human and artificial, but words must never ebb and flow; they must a crucial stasis be. The most frightening thought-ghost of all.

Yet, these words I know to be mine and mine only are also uncertain. The solid dependable ghost or gestalt, you see, remains to be captured by the additional means of an as yet unknown 'shadowy third'.

And so we hunt on. Around every groyne and wave-blocker. Along every shaft of light reaching the reached-out eye below the makeshift roofs and dark attics of our head.

THE VERTICAL EYE

Despite smiling with stoical forbearance for most of my life, well, at least smiling inwardly, the scares and frights were never really over. I had been led into a sense of false security or dire failure, whichever way one chose to look at it, by a series of disappointing ghosts that cancelled out the earlier shudders induced even by the pointing ghost, indeed, by the painting one, too, yes, most of my hunting's finds were disappointing ghosts, not really cutting the mustard in the scheme of being able to establish them for real as a result of hunting for them in the first place. (By the way, I remind myself that I shall later tell you of one particular Disappointing Ghost that deserves a story all of its own.)

Disappointing ghosts, you see, are usually just that, especially when they pass through our lives without our really noticing their tenuous presence, although sometimes glimpsed out of the corner of the eye with the most minor of frissons felt.

That 'corner of the eye' cliché meantime somehow reminds me that I was once a ghost-hunting nerd, who manufactured ghosts from the slightest suspicion of one, from the most outlandish of forced pareidolia or the most unconnectable of connections or the most unsynchronous of synchronicities or the most forgotten of dreams, thus striving to bolster the manufactured ghost into more than it was. But as I grew older, the ghosts I found in 'found art' as well as fine art, and in literature and music, were more defined, more likely to unflesh out into real spectral existence, but so far never quite managing it, never *quite* crystallising into *the* ghost I ever sought.

I had, however, high hopes for the ghost that I named 'The Vertical Eye', whereby a fleeting moment of an eye's 'smiling' joy and a pathetic teardrop perfectly blended, therefore nourishing the belief that this was the Real McCoy. It was a mild ghost, yes, but it seemed to be a real one to nail down and then flag as a success for my ghost-hunting Curriculum Vitae. But instead it managed to nail *me* down and then shook what was left of me in its own random winds of induced fate, whereby I needed to disown its capture completely by blocking it without even knowing why I needed to do so, and putting myself in undeniable denial, so that I could then forget it had ever existed at all. Except I do recall there remain several visual mementos of it in the book entitled '*Weirdmonger: The Nemonicon: The Synchronised Shards of Random Truth and Fiction*' (2003) which thankfully nearly everybody, including me, fails even to look inside, let alone read for real.

Yet, I am suddenly aware, in real-time, that a version of the Vertical Eye coldly stares at anyone who happens simply to skim or take a quick look at this story as well as at anyone who closely reads it in full. Just cast your eye to the right-hand side of this text! Or in some cases below it.

THE SHADOWY THIRD

I really must not allow this recent gushing of new fiction works to return to its erstwhile dribble, but, as they say, the inevitable truths that fiction contains will inevitably out!

So, as would-be fiction writer again, rather than the ghost-hunter manqué, I took myself, upon a trip seeking writerly inspiration, to the annual Convention of Pareidoliacs in Ipswich. I had never attended a previous one, so I was staggered at the array of trestle tables displaying various attendees' prized items, some with photographs depicting cloudscapes and such, others with physical objects, vegetable and mineral, that took the evident shape of what they were not. A painting called 'The Stalking Horse' was the most popular item, and I wish I could reproduce it here, but cameras were banned in the Convention hall.

I attended some of the early lectures and talked to many attendees who struck me as not as odd as I had predicted, even perhaps not as odd as me. And I now began to see myself as a practising pareidoliac, a sense of self that was consistent with ghost hunting and its branch-line of dream-catching. But when I met a man called Douglas — a dapperly dressed man in a monocle and plus fours — I found myself listening to his tales of animal taxidermy as a form of pareidolia. He was later due to give a lecture on this very subject.

I do not know why I have attempted there to give the start of a character study with regard to Douglas, as our acquaintanceship was short-lived and I later forgot about his lecture in favour of another event when many of the attendees collected in the town's Butter Market to scry the buildings in a session of mass pareidolia.

But, of course, this is all fiction. Just a sleight of hand, a prestidigitation of writing to defeat a dearth of words otherwise. My mind was elsewhere most of the time dealing with my own true vocation of spectral and spectator research, as yet unfulfilled, while I followed two people I had befriended at the convention, now turning their heads in the Butter Market as if they had sensed a ghost behind them. Or as if they had seen, from the corner of the eye, a human body as shaped from nothing, an entity striving poignantly to fit itself into some pantomime horse of existential believability or potential outing of truth from within, indeed as the very thing it sought or actually sought to be. An internal scrying. Or the flippetygibbet of a stopgap between other roles, if truth be known.

THE DISAPPOINTING GHOST

As promised, here it is. A ghost story with a ghost that belies the title I have just given it! And maybe that is all I need to write.Indeed, I may regret writing more. In the end, I should have left it hanging there, just as I did when writing about the ghost in 'The Third Bed'!

But to take this beyond just a tantalising legerdemain of narration, the next ghost — that I *almost* established and to which I have assigned the above name — has ever since threatened in my mind to turn up again and prove itself wholly or holistically as an entire entity without the need of that italicised word. And the time has come, here, now, with a real-time witnessing of a story title overturned.

You see, I have been ghost hunting in and around the Jumbo Water Tower in Colchester, an area which, with sudden second thoughts now thought too late, should have remained nameless, in case you all flock there to check out this ghost.

Ghost hunters, you see, can be pretty ruthless, often counterproductive to the cause or course of actually producing an established and checked-out paranormal apparition, often acting as if they are performing a trick as a tour de force in the stage act that life has become, with any established ghost now likely to be revealed before the very eyes of millions, a viral act of self-defeat in a world of trending media, because any real ghost, believe me, all too readily dissolves into little more than mucky residues in the gutter when placed under the strain of such enormous scrutiny.

So, there you have it. I should have left it with the two short sentences above at outset. I promise the next story I shall write will be not only a real story with believable characters, but one with a ghost *also* capable of being deemed as such. (No wonder old ghost stories often had placenames replaced with just an initial and a dash.)

AS TEXTED LATE AT NIGHT TO A RANDOM RECIPIENT

Back to the mansions, as well as to the hopefully haunted churches, a somewhat expected path judging by my more recent stories, but for the first time I find myself treading along it towards both at once.

I top the hill with my hiking boots just as the sun is setting and discern two mansions and two churches close to some afforestation that appear to be unmapped by Google but self-evidently (because I had started off that morning hiking there!) within the precincts of Suffolk, not far from Rendlesham. You see, I usually enjoyed not knowing where I was going and where I was due to stay the night and did not even carry a tent because I simply knew serendipity and weather were usually my friends amidst such voluntary directionlessness — unless I was forced to break such a rule when becoming out so late, darkness being its own weather, and still without a roof to cover me.

Neither of the mansions appear to be hotels; the churches, too close to each other for comfort, are obviously last resorts even when given the kindness of a friendly priest, curate, verger or sexton. I have no illusions. This was no longer the era of Walter de la Mare. I now admit I was often disappointed by my own serendipity at the end of the day.

There are a few odd houses scattered between the two mansions, one of which mansions, close-up in the dying light, appears to be quite roofless in its unwelcome. Many of the houses roofless, too, it seems. Except one. The second mansion at the other end of the 'High Street' does appear to maintain a roof, but all its windows appear permanently shuttered.

I turn my attention towards the two churches set back from the so-called street, both almost sunk into the trees that seem to have grown taller with the equal sinking of the sun. One church with a spire, the other with a tower. A bit worse for wear. Or for lack of worshipers in a thinly crowded market for them. Collection plates must go spare here, I assume.

But I need characters to bolster my story, and I soon realise that I don't need to create them out of thin air, because a few actually appear, as if on magical cue, at the door of the sole house that has kept its roof. Evidently, strangers were a curiosity hereabouts, and, from their point of view, I, as pilgrim, was the stranger, not them, of course.

"Anywhere to stay?" I ask, while pointing meaningfully at the darkening sky.

A woman about my age stays silent, as if that's answer enough.

A younger man with whom she evidently counts herself to be an 'item', does say something or other that I do not catch, and if this were fiction, I would no doubt have concocted something audible for him to say. Which proves something, I suppose.

The third individual with a dog is of indeterminate gender under a thick coat, someone whom I would get to know better. But at this point, my guess is as good as yours.

"Where am I?" I'm evidently trying to make small talk. If only there had been a pub, pub talk being the best ice-breaker of all.

The dog now starts barking at me as if in answer to my question. It's not aggressive barking. I think this dog to be the nearest thing to being real in the whole place, as a consequence of its apparent readiness to respond.

But, then, I notice what I have hoped all along to meet since arriving here, a single friendly-seeming churchman approaching our group from the church with a spire. I try with squinted eye to see exactly how friendly, and I am reassured by an almost vertical smile from between chubby chops and above a bright white dog-collar, as this item of ecclesiastical regalia is often impolitely called. I hold out a hand along with my own version of his smile.

He's followed, though, by another and another friendly churchman. And soon there is the start of more churchmen spilling from the other church with a tower. All of them emanating friendliness, but the fact there are so many of these churchmen — all seeming to be as friendly as churchmen usually are in wayside places such as this — should be seen as a part of a single pattern of meaning, in a place complete, I now see, with graveyards and much stone-etched text to scry from headstones at late evening. This mass overfriendliness causes the individual with a dog to take me by the elbow and lead me to the shuttered mansion for shelter. Whether we reach it in time I need to leave to the responsibility of serendipity to decide. I wonder whether this mansion will furnish any rooms to stay in at all and whether the roofless mansion would be a better bet. Or would both, between them, present a vast gutted space… My phone gutters, too, now upon the cusp of its dead point of having run out of power. A sort of convivial hospitality source with the shrunkest bar imaginable. And the dog is dead already.

THE GHOST HANGAR

As that of a ghost hunter, dreamcatcher, author, reviewer, publisher, pareidoliac, electronic-photosynthesist and mnemonic-beachcomber, my daily constitutional for some years has been from Holland on Sea where I have lived for many years towards Clacton Pier, starting out at the Queensway ZigZag slopes that featured recently in my Nightjar publication 'The Birthday Presence' and now proceeding with, ahead, the familiar haunting sight of the pier sporting its closeness to the silhouette of a Ferris wheel and bearing itself a helterskelter and other rides alongside inferred buzzing amusement arcades, a pier whose actual own outline echoes those of the Essex Serpents disguised as rock-sculpted groynes leading up to the pier, as I walk. A magical journey on foot, keeping Mortality hungry at some distant corner of time, perhaps till an ever encroaching 'now'.

Recently, though, it is not a surprise that some of my ghost hunting ambitions are increasingly bearing fruit. Just yesterday I witnessed the three haunted and hooded figures, plodding one behind the other, as if from some distant Zeno-trod war, proceeding along beside the deepest blue sea I have ever seen since living here, as followed by a small orange boat upon the richly coloured sea beside them. I knew then that tomorrow (which is now today) would be Airshow Day here, weather permitting. Somehow, I had reached some apotheosis of ghost hunting, but the ghost hunter stood still.

Not yet, he said, surely not yet. And he thought of some other living names to add to those in 'Alone With the Horrors', these perhaps deserving a nod of obeisance for their actions if not only for their work alone, or both equally, or just one of these two aspects, viz., in no particular order, Wamack, (Kirk S.) King, Tullis, (Jason) Smith, (Garrie) Hall, (Sue) Harper, Straker, Veres, O'Driscoll, Cox, VanderMeer, Ostermeier, Schaller, Wehunt, Jeffery, Hughes, Rothermel, Toase, Nurrish, Nogle, Ghahwagi and more such names no doubt saved for later in this series of stories. And I thought again of the buzzing amusement arcades, and compared them to the old fashioned ones I haunted as a child while accompanying my Mum in the early 1950s, with my having been born near Walton on Naze pier in a seaside town that recently hosted the scene of the Third Bed syndrome within this concurrent canon of fiction, but perhaps not so much able to be called fiction as the hunted and haunted ghost awaiting around the corner, a turning that one seems ever to fail reaching. Time to watch the planes. One of them will sure to be a ghost, too, as it opens a second set of angel-like wings while shedding its first set with a synchronous splash below in a sea that has grown grey since yesterday. I just need one old penny for a mechanical toy crane to turn the handle of which an impossible prize will hang.

WHY DON'T WE DO IT IN THE ROAD?

One of the first ghosts I almost established was in the late 1960s when living in the seaside resort of Morecambe, Lancashire, while a young student attending the nearby University at Bailrigg. And it was in fact the latter placename — and perhaps I should have replaced it with an initial and a dash, as in many ghost stories of yore — that triggered much in my life with its wordplay aura of rescue by arty installation and/or by happening and hoax or even by the sea's wandering ghostly vessel that I never saw for real till yesterday as reported in the previous story. And believe me, I did need rescuing in those youthful times. But that is merely backdrop to the real ghost story I now wish to tell for the first time.

As some of you may know, Morecambe has Northern grit, with an ambiance of stand-up comedy and dance halls with ageing couples slowly twirling to the scrape and tunefulness of Palm Court strings. And a potentially lethal bay, instead of a sea proper, although sea it surely was.

I lived along with the White Album in a tall terraced house that had seen better times, wherein holidaying folk stayed whenever the students returned to their parental homes. The landlady, Mrs Gill, was a force to reckon with, as was the garish wallpaper. Not so much a pale yellow wallpaper for the slow diminishment of my body and spirit, but a tasteless jagged retreat to times when modernity was a future nightmare but people still seemed to want to emulate it in the guise of a projected nostalgia of what we were all due to lose sooner or later. I knew not how to write even then, as you can see, but I still managed to erect essays of study that both haunted and hoaxed my tutors at Bailrigg. And thus, despite some sporadic sinking setbacks, I finished with a commendable level of achieved degree, as also helped by the support of my then future wife whom I met at Bailrigg and who stayed in digs nearby in Morecambe.

So much for the brand of truth that acts as backdrop to this story, I must move on now to a different truth that is fiction. I met a ghost one night during one of the most sunk periods for my vessel of life. Unless this, too, is a constructed hoax, it derived from attending a concert at the Winter Gardens where Alan Price was performing a set, having left the Animals. I now wish the ghost sighting had been a happening at the brashly atonal extravaganza I earlier or later attended within the late 1960s, it being a gig by Cornelius Cardew mainly bashing a piano in relentless rhythm like a future Philip Glass on steroids, an event taking place in one of the churches of Lancaster that served as temporary university space while quite large amounts of Bailrigg were still being built around the students who stayed and studied there. A church was meant to contain a ghost, after all. But, no, as I have said already, the ghost was connected to my visit to the Morecambe Winter Gardens on its Pop Music night, with a dark wintry Northern night outside, thus attracting locals more than any residual day-trippers. Students, other than myself and a few others, were sparse there, too. I have no colluding witness for my truth or for my hoax. Most people there that night are now dead, I guess, or huddled together with different ghosts elsewhere without thought of why their consciousness may still have survived until now.

I idled outside the Winter Gardens while smoking, despite the fact that I could have in those days smoked inside it, and I discerned a large vessel floundering upon the deceiving currents of the completely dark bay, only visible because the vessel was darker than darkness.

"What do you think that is?" I heard a voice ask rhetorically. I turned to see a shape that could well be human, even if the voice didn't sound as if it was human at all. This shape smoked, too. Those were the days when everyone and everything smoked like chimneys. I managed to give up the habit gradually throughout the ensuing years, so you now know I must have survived long enough to do that, despite what happened to me on that night of which I tell. Sorry for removing all suspense from my story by making that fact clear. Yet something happened that makes even such certainty on my part as vulnerable as the vessel I thought I saw that night upon the bay. Maybe a hoax, maybe a hex, maybe simply a trick of fiction as truth. It was a devastating huge blast against all the vulnerable vessels I contained, a single blast of all the future music that I was destined to hear, often by choice during the rest of my life, all here in an unimaginable 'mix', a fell synchronised concatenation of various premonitions and styles to choose from, before they happened. Just as a deep darkness stood out by dint of an even deeper darkness, or vice versa, the vast cacophony stood outlined against itself, too. Inside the Winter Gardens, Alan Price sang on. Simon Smith and his Amazing Dancing Bear. Remember it's all just fiction. Except for Mrs Gill, the wallpaper and the Glass Onion. And maybe more.

THE GLASS ONION

The ghost furthest from being a ghost, as it happened to be after hunting and then finding it, was unworthy of even the word 'almost' a ghost, and it featured during a lengthy sojourn with my young family on the Clockhouse Mount during the whole of Thatcher's era into Major's. My contemporaneous horror stories, if not ghost stories, featuring this place can be easily found by any enthusiast on one of my websites.

It was so far from being a ghost, it ceased to be anything at all. Until hindsight kicked in, that is. The pub called The Jack and Jill — which I rediscovered, making a small diversion to see it when I was driven past the area upon one of those life-guzzling motorways that connect places today — is still there, even if almost a derelict shell of itself. And the man who once cut my hair was seen snipping away at an unseen customer. Now much older, he still traded behind the same window of the same depressing shopping façade.

Memories welled up in me, like little rodent ghosts nibbling away at their past reality. Yet, I was mainly happy in this place, I remember, for many reasons I need not expand on here. There are some who shared my happiness there who have the same memories, if filtered differently. Very important people in my life, such as those to whom I read nursery rhymes, as well as the walk-on parts of those with whom I worked in nearby deepest Surrey, and the workaday actors who shared the creaky stage with me in the Amateur Dramatics at Clockhouse's Hillcrest Hall. And, of course, in the tradition of Reggie Oliver's ghost stories, in that latter place, the ghost, about which I speak above, once resided. The ghost was, I think, most of all present when we performed a certain play — a farce called 'The Glass Onion', by a forgotten playwright — but was otherwise indescribable, even worth not mentioning at all. The ghost *and* the play.

Although this ghost was as attenuated as far as attenuation can reach without being nothing at all, it still haunts me with even more than the horror I left behind in the guise of the ludicrous horror stories written back there and that nobody ever reads, including me. Almost-nothing-at-all is quite unnoticeable, you see, when it secretes itself in a pocket, stowing-away as it were, when I moved house by means of those damnable motorways to the distant Essex seaside, as it must have done in hindsight. It whispers silently, you see, as I ever write Beyond Credence.

HALF HOAX, HALF HEX

I learnt some lessons today from a book review just this minute finished, which review, you may ask, well, it's for me to know, and for you to find out. These stories, meantime, are half truth, half fiction, often with an established backstory, to give some substance to the scares, and to bolster the hidden codes (hidden is a better word, than occult), codes that my attempted wordplay deploys disingenuously but with some skills hopefully of reality-erection and ghost-establishment in an otherwise scatterbrained hunting for such things. They scare me, you see, so I expect they will scare you, too.

My established backstory today, is that of Hastings, Sussex, where I spent a few summer holidays in the 1960s with my grandmother who lived there on West Hill at that time. A wonderful place of vast views of the New Town and mazy Old Town bookshops and East Hill's rough country where Pitch and Putt prevailed, as well as the sight of the Dolphin building whose Witch Doctor disco I attended, too, and, if memory serves, you could discern distant Beachy Head where people died. But my story takes place in next door St. Leonard's where the old buildings half-soar, mentally half-squat, with digs galore within them, and there is the seasoned age and imposing awe of inland town and seaside resort merged, and where ghosts are sure to abound, as a certain unexpected ghost did that day when I, a ghost hunter rookie in the 1960s, visited there for no reason at all. Just to get out of my Nanna's hair I guess, as she thought me too much of a homebird and spoilt by her daughter who happened to be my mother back in Colchester.

It was not an obvious ghost, it was more a Close Encounter of the one and a half kind with a huge hovering UFO that nobody saw but me, judging by the expressionless faces of the bent and the upstanding streetwalkers alike and holidaymakers who had lost their bearings. It reared above a terraced shop's upper frontage, a UFO as mass of uncertain resemblance to anything that can be described, with more ancient flashing colours upon its silver bulk than the Witch Doctor itself (in those days Psychedelia was as basic as lights going on and off to the sound of Little Stevie Wonder as he was then known) but this was a future Virtual Reality show to kill something at root in your soul. And things trooped from a vertical eye-shape in the UFO's flank (now a UFO landed as a ULO) onto the roof, indeed one of those many roofs invisible to ground-level eyes, even if you actually thought to raise the sight sufficiently to notice what the tops of buildings in otherwise run-of-the-mill towns sported as codes of found art or etched engravings too far-fetched to read. These things must have found it difficult to walk on such roofs even if the roof slopes were not steep enough to see, or if not roofs there at all, such things vanishing into the terraced mansions below them. I use the word 'walk' advisedly, as these things I call 'things' did not appear to have legs. Nor did my belief in them have legs at all, however suspended my disbelief was eventually to become as I continued to watch them.

These ‘things’, however, before my belief in them finally vanished, did emerge from their sunk-roof syndrome with what seemed to be an old woman in a particular thing’s ‘arms’, but she did not seem distressed as far as I could tell. It was as if a moment of truth or proof had happened for once in this duplicitous world that was merely incubating itself in those just past the mid-century days of which I speak. I lowered my eyes for a moment, too, as if in respectful obeisance to something I did not understand and when I lifted them again, all was as it had been before what later happened.

A bent old woman undeniably standing next to me on the pavement smiled a near vertical smile at me and went her way, as did some others, even a holidaymaker who seemed to be in the know about some different code to mine, and, later that day, I returned to my temporary West Hill home, with its widest view possible of countless New Town roofs as well as the cricket ground and the railway station, went home, indeed, to my then much younger Nanna. And I, for once, felt Rhagarol, and the world my oyster.

FRINTON'S FRONT

Quite close to where I live in Holland on Sea is posh Frinton on Sea, well, I have managed to walk there at a push, until recently. Past the Haven's radar mast, striding, or perhaps shambling in more recent days, along the sea wall onward to Frinton golf course, and eventually the town's enclave itself where in wartime days my Mum worked for the Naafi. And in later years, a place that did not allow pubs, fish-and-chips nor buses to enter its precinct. I think it has relaxed a bit since, if a place can relax, rather than the people who live there.

H. Russell Wakefield, one of the great ghost story writers of all times, mentioned Frinton at least twice in his fiction, and so it may already have a readiness to be a venue for strange thoughts and even stranger sightings. But when I once spotted the church, the smallest in Essex, I believe, I sensed that ghost hunting would not go amiss in and around it. But that was in the days when I had not fully seen my métier for what it was and Frinton's front was impermeable to me. But the church being quite close to the main shopping area, Connaught Avenue, one would have thought anything supernaturally eerie would be unlikely to happen. Not ripe for my quirky amateurish ghost hunting, as it was then (and perhaps Frinton itself had not yet fully fulfilled such a magnetic role, too, in this context), even though my quirkiness was a mask for something more deeply unsettling than I could then imagine. And indeed I often found Frinton unsettling, despite its happy wide beaches with old-fashioned wooden groynes that had been replaced with rocky fishtails where I lived myself, and Frinton's plush beach huts worthy of bigger constructions, ladders and outcrops of wooden backramps et al. And a shop that seemed to be a girl's wardrobe. And a little park on the sea front with a tree carved into a sharp beaky bird, with a castle gate hewn into its base. Not forgetting the imposingly well-named Grand Hotel of Frinton facing the round clock-shelter on the sea front's upper green, a shelter that looked like a morphing from a time-travelling Tardis vehicle. The whole place seemed made for me. Both chirpy and unsettling, as I think I may have implied during these ramblings on my part. I can supply photographs if required. No rooms with spare third beds in these large houses and mansions hereabouts, rooms large enough to be single-minded and en suite, only to be shared when required. Sometimes, I wondered about just one room filling some of the town's mansions. Duties as missing attics and lofts left for the owner's beach huts to fulfil, especially in the off-season. But now I seem to be rambling off piste.

I simply must focus on my tale, if only for my mother's sake, who spent most of her earlier years in Essex living on a boathouse called the 'Onward' as moored amid the Walton-on-the-Naze backwaters, where Arthur Ransome set some of his Swallows and Amazons adventures. As a child, I preferred Enid Blyton, though. And Biggles at a push. Which brings me back to that outing on foot I once took from Holland to Frinton along with an old walking friend, now sadly deceased, whose mind was as wandering as now my own mind possibly wanders even worse than his did then.

We saw Frinton in the distance as we left Holland Haven, and our proposed destination suddenly appeared to be an enticingly magical place over the brow of its own golf course, in the golden shafts of something that was not sun-bred. The shafts came from a direction in the sky, in fact, different from where the sun was meant to be.

Golden as in something to be wished for.

But there were bigger fish to fend off. And the sea shimmered not with the rich blue I described earlier in these storified reports of mine, but a deep yellow that, despite such dark deepness, blinded our eyes. We managed to hasten onward, onward being a word I cannot escape using in this context, and I shrugged off something my friend seemed to accept as natural as I helped lead him to the promised land of a later pub lunch in Walton which we would reach if we could walk that far, indeed plugging on towards Walton's vast tiers of beach huts near its long pier and near where I was conceived, Walton being where we always intended to be rather than in Frinton, a plan that all along entailed our desire to by-pass Frinton despite the length of the walk we would be forced to strain our ageing sinews to achieve, and much of what I have written above was to give that very false impression of our intentions to visit a place called Frinton that lay in wait for us, but by now it had discovered this my deceitful narration and was pulling us onward towards that small church inside its gates, a church that I mentioned before. Or was it the beaky bird that called us or the clock shelter cowering before a huge hotel with not guestrooms inside but a vast inner space gutted bigger even than the Tardis itself?

I can't ask my friend now. But I am pretty sure we only escaped by pretending that we never intended to leave Holland at all, and with some boyish laughter and relief we turned back at the point in our walk where we always turned back, just as Holland became Frinton at the front edge of the latter's golf course where stick-like figures with sticks they swung seemed to wave at us.

We even joked that we were auditioning for a new series of 'Last of the Summer Wine' and we sought the actual number 42 in various configurations, too, just as a game to bypass time. He thought these were my jokes, but little did he know how serious I could be. And I turned round to glimpse the Frinton we had escaped (or did it, for reasons of its own, relax its hold on us?) and I saw with some relief that the sky had returned to pale blue, and the sea an even richer blue than I had ever seen it before. This story is merely now my aide memoire never to forget such events in honour of my friend. Pity I did not write it earlier when maybe it would not have been so wandering in its focus. And who knows, if we had reached Frinton, I may have found the very ghost that has ever eluded my hunting for it. Or does it hunt me, instead? Who or what is the front line we both defend?

THE THIN KING

I have achieved little success so far in this canon of 'stories' to hunt out the real ghost that all ghost hunters seek to find, with erected holo-words filled up by codes as to such a ghost's undeniable existence, while also bolstered by the truths of an author's personal past life intrinsic to such stories as well as attempts at deploying the interspersed power of fiction itself to further, even more, such bolstering of the truths by lateral thinking, but the goal remains elusive, permanently tantalised by the brinkmanship of attainment. So try other means, I say. Strip a story of its setting, its set of people, its backstory, its plot and place, even its set of words, even losing a rare odd letter or two along the way, that would have couched any non-events' onward course towards an ending. But these words that I use to express my intentions are words themselves, you claim, that I am using for you to read about them! And I shrug my shoulders and so plan to resort to all those missing ingredients of a story yet again.

But GHOST stories surely do not logically exist by definition of what I fear can never be hunted down.

So there you have it, and my goal is finally reached. A philosophical impossibility made possible by fiction's fearless force. A conundrum beaten out to the extra rhythms of Azathoth's celebratory flutes and violins. Here, then, as necessary non sequitur, is the next story in line set out, as tempered by a restraint not demonstrated above. Meantime, it seems I have hunted down the ghost I sought during a lifetime of seeking it, simply by twisting a thought one ratchet further than I had ever twisted it before. 'Torque Stories', the would-be overall title of this still evolving collection of short-short ghost stories, to supplement a volume called 'Gauche Stories' that is currently planned to be published independently before the end of my life, that in turn will supplement the already published volumes entitled 'Dabbling With Diabelli' and 'A Man Too Mean to be Me' that were published following 'The Last Balcony' and 'Weirdmonger' before *them*. I have several more stories to tell, I hope, as a mass debriefing for now such a lifelong hunting's sudden success. Thinking about it, to debrief a series of short-shorts is to make them longer, I guess. Thinking about such things again and again, perhaps forever, before the story proper shows its face.

Once upon a time, there was a thin King who doubted his own thoughts, despite the apparent worship his subjects demonstrated for each of his proclamations. His fairy tale castle resided in a world that sparkled less than some fantasy of yore, yet never so grim as Grimm either! These subjects, however, pretended to obey his words while doing their own thing without him knowing. The complete opposite happens between ruler and ruled in our own real world, you may already have noticed! But this is not a fable with a moral, but a fiction for its own sake, so please do not expect an easy message massaging your prejudices as you squat with your constant rage inside now legendary roofless and roomless mansions.

This thin King was the sort who knew more about dealing with whoever read about him in a story about him than he knew about his subjects themselves within the story, subjects who had objectively never been taught to read beyond words of one syllable. His future bride, to be wed to him when she eventually came of rage, was a case in point with regard to the one-syllable syndrome, so his preliminary love letters written to her in the guise of ghost hunting stories went mainly to waste. So, she thought him to be some waster who wrote nothing but nonsense extending its various lengths *null immortalis*. PS I love you. Fat or not.

A VENETIAN TALE

Getting back to basics, allow me to explain that, for the ten years between 1975 and 1985, I wrote very little creative fiction material, yet as a character I appeared in stories written by unnamed sources and placed in plot venues I had not yet visited in real life. Towards the end of the century into the noughties, however, I travelled throughout Europe with my wife on coach tours, and thus I eventually managed to fulfil the visit to a particular city that my character had already made in the following story from years before…

Venice saw the arrival of the ghost hunter who had English and Welsh roots. His name was ever unclear except for the epithet I have already given him. He tried to remain incognito as he believed such a state of tenuous existence as a person enabled an easier approach to supernatural phenomena who would be less suspiciously frightened of him if without a name and a passport. How he had reached Venice, in such insubstantial circumstances, still remains a mystery. He mainly sought, he told locals, a ghost that was substantial enough to dress in real clothes. But that, in hindsight, I realised was an ironical claim, to conceal his real purposes.

There was a ghost that fitted very few labels or pre-conditions, about which it had been bruited in British paranormal circles as being one that haunted the canals of Venice while seeking very old locals who might remember a literary man and an unconnected youth both of whom once stayed there during a cholera outbreak, the latter youth accompanying a well-to-do family. But, in the end, I guess, they were a different older man and younger man the ghost sought than those who seemed obvious from the original terms of its reputed quest. Men that somehow crossed continents without official papers, too.

Indeed, the ghost hunter stumbled upon a different ghost altogether from any yet discussed, on a night of masked celebration for the city, a ghost wearing a mask with one slit not seeming to cover a proper face at all. I shudder even now at the thought. A vertical eye staring into the night, if the mask's single slit was deduced correctly.

Which brings me to the nub of the night around which this story circles in uncertain currents. The ghost hunter was accustomed for his research to what we call mansions in Britain, readily generous as they were with many almost-ghosts, as I call them, but the Venetian form of these mansions were called palazzos, their roofs mainly still intact but their foundations sunk deep in the surrounding canals with often rank and real mucky water. The ghost hunter wondered about the nature of the rooms inside the palazzos and how residents managed irrigation or ablution and eventual drainage. Commodes, he thought, must have been the answer.

A rising damp, too, he feared, a feeling that made his own bones seem to seep. Attics would be the safest place to hunt, if he could gain permission to enter them. Without a name, though, real people had more suspicion of him than he had assumed any potential ghosts apparently to have. Gondoliers were fussy, too, not taking any passenger without any checking, yet the ghost hunter was later poled, on a gondola with a single lantern, nearer to a particular incontinent palazzo, but a palazzo chosen by whom? This gondolier, who had agreed to take him in the end, was masked with a mask barely sufficient to see through to know where he was going. The water splashed with deceptively subtle tones of flute and violin, despite or because their respective holes and strings were slack or clogged, in contrast to the ghost hunter's guilty heart beating, as he stood up precariously in the gondola under a quickly expunged crevice of the lantern's light, indeed drumming as loudly as when the heart itself — while I was peering at his swaying shape with my vultural eye — had been snatched, upon its first drumming, from below a nearby Palazzo's sunken floor.

THE TINIEST MANSION OF ALL

Any house, however basic-gaslit-1950s-bijou-cosy-needing-repair as it was then, with a toilet outside and no bathroom, can seem to be a mansion when an inhabitant who lives there magnifies its essential wonders. Time indeed now takes me back to Old Heath Road days, post Walton on Naze, having now moved to a terraced house slope-straightened upon a hill and next door to another such house that had then been turned into a small grocery selling sweets, a corner shop plumped in the middle of a long line of houses, just opposite the end of Scarletts Road that led to Colchester's Recreation Ground... well, the more I reminisce, the more the story will be lost. But I am first forced to tell you about these school days of mine that involved St George's Junior an imaginary enemy-filled walk away in Canterbury Road and later the Grammar School a two-wheeler bike ride away, as pedalled via the Army Garrison precinct roads.
At the back of our house was a long thin garden containing a bullace tree in the branches of which I often sat wearing a Davy Crockett hat, and then further back some rough ground which the council later built up by means of cranes and diggers into a higher mound for new housing, and even further off, before the new houses arrived, two poplar trees, as iconic memories of those days, one tree taller than the other. Outside trundled past the No. 6 bus into town plus the equivalent, in the 1950s, of the wi-fi hub I dreamt to be

under the pavement just in front of our gate. My parents often at the Hippodrome Bingo having given up the black and white films they used to watch in Walton's place for moving pictures. And me, when a little older, here in Colchester, watching the Dambusters film at the Embassy Cinema with daylight showing through its roof in echo now of something else I can't now quite nail down. And much more from those days slides away even before I know it is there to grab, with no possible grounds for recreation.

With these pictures of the Old Heath Road locale now set in words, I find — especially at my age of such slippage — that the story I intended to tell has indeed been lost with no memory of it connected to one or more of those careful images from my past, including a ghost to feature in it actually to turn it into a ghost story, indeed *the* ghost I have ever since written about hunting and never found. A ghost story — that has vanished even before any chance to read it, or to write it, or even, in hindsight, to think it at all — is strangely the most frightening ghost story of all.

NIGHTMARE'S WOMB

In the early to mid Seventies, the ghost hunter worked in Pall Mall near the National Gallery and later at a building erected upon the Temple of Mithras within the City of London near the dome of St. Paul's, much of which appeared in the ghost hunter's then written-down dreams.

Many of you will know of the potential for ghosts in the mazy byways of those parts of London, but the ghost hunter also wandered into the streets of Whitechapel and Shadwell. And that was when Canary Wharf was still in its mine before being hawled out in earth-blasting array. Meanwhile, this is the start of a new series of Torque Tales as yet to be written from that direction of penmanship.

St Paul's, of course, was the nub of such things, if I can be relatively blunt about the ghost hunter's spiritually magnetic compass, which I suppose makes sense as that cathedral, in whatever stage of evolution, has been intended from outset to be a centre of a *form* of spirituality, if not necessarily the ghost hunter's own form. The paintings in the gallery also carried a forcefield of spectral punch. And this first tale in the new series implies a hand-twisted arch between the tip of the famous dome and one particular painting in the gallery that memory has veiled, whatever the distance needed to be plied between them. Not like the straddling cathedral in 'Agra Aska' that some of you may already know, because that was in an alternate world. These tales take place in our own perceived world of reality, even if it may be someone's else alternate one! The ghost hunter took reality for granted in all their dealings with it. Even if their hunting's eventual gestalt was gaslit like an ancient *version* of the city they now walked.

This is both an introduction to such a series of tales and a tale in itself. With scene setting comments as well as a beginning, middle and end, even if there is no 'found ghost' to speak of and no climax as yet to satisfy any avid reader of ghost stories. But I sense there is a slight pervasive frisson of fear for you to harbour in hope or even dread of such frisson's future growth into nightmare. Until it fades like this print itself.

BOOK-KEEPING

I worked at my desk with a giant calculator looking like a cash register with many buttons and a large handle to turn, working with many others in the same open-plan place, clattering away during those mid-century days. So typical of offices then. No accounting for such humdrum existences.

There is an Early Netherlandish portrait (1434), an oil painting of the marriage of a couple on an oak panel, with a strange mirror behind them reflecting the scene in an oblique manner. And I often stared at it during my lunch-breaks away from calculators, with my having skirted, before arriving at the gallery, the Trafalgar Square and its imposing column with what appeared to be a sculptural depiction of a human being on top, but it was too far to see who it was. I won't dwell on that for long, as you can already see where I am going with it, no doubt.

It's the painting in the gallery I want to concentrate upon — and I certainly did during those early days of my career, the gorgeous green of the woman's dress making her appear 'with child'. The man in a black wide-brimmed hat and dark cape raises a hand in blessing, as if he is the priest exercising the necessary rituals to marry themselves! I won't name them. No-one is to be named in these stories, for fear of unwanted truths being wrenched from the lips of too many people with more information than they need to know, especially when gentle persuasion turns into ugly torture. We're heading in that general direction, I guess, today!

I dreamt one night during the period of watching this painting, and as I found myself concentrating on the painting, its colours were now dripping muckily over its frame. Greens and blacks in some outer melting abstraction. I yearned to return to the office and to the ordinary people there who worked their lives away as clerks in mindless tasks and large paper ledgers. It seemed more comforting to be with them than in this dream. But when arriving at the exit/entrance to leave, I saw the gallery's famous columns were now tall caryatids barring my way each with one vertical eye patched over.

I woke in a sweat. I feared it might become a recurring dream, one with serial potential beyond its original ending. I was thankfully moved from that office soon afterwards to a different one within the same firm, and it was near St Paul's Cathedral. They called it a promotion to a customer-facing role rather than backroom handle-grinder and number-cruncher. The cathedral, when I visited it the first lunchtime, turned out to have many more columns than was good for it, radiating, as it did, nether regions or heavenly ones. And, in my head, with some creative accounting, I calculated who was eventually to be married there. I shall keep them nameless.

ONE DROGULUS TOO FAR

The ghost hunter once wrote down their thoughts from dreams in what what was then later called their 'first published story entitled Padgett Weggs', named after a title of a piece of music they had improvised and recorded on cassette earlier — in which 'story' was featured the dome of St Paul's crawling all over with Old Ones. Now, ironically, they are an Old One themselves. We are, too.

I am, I think, more than simply empathetic with such Oldness. And pronouns need their nails cutting, as you know too well.

In that first 'story', Weggs found his mother dead in a septic tank, I recall. I would need to reread the rest of it about him and her, since the rest is forgotten. And also its immediate sequels need to be reread, too. And now today, around 40 years later, I write this latest sequel that could never have been predicted as being possible to exist, because of the potentially lethal hurdles of planet and personal self between then and now. A relatively long period of time, indeed, until now when everyone is a pronoun of choice, and we can only fully give names to people who are fictional characters.

A twist of destiny as one watches the dreams unfold again and again, many of them each night, between bouts of necessary waking. A Drogulus here, a Drogulus there, instead of the real ghost one ever sought but cannot find, they're on the landing outside the room of three beds, and each of them finds itself to be between a ceiling and a stairwell. And in the background one hears the music of flutes, drums and violins approaching nearer and nearer, as story follows story like levels in a mansion that towers with attic space to spare. No label of Babel, it just is.

And, so, life itself that one needs to live so as to write the stories that creates the life that created them in the first place, will be sure to prevail perhaps forever, whoever the one is whom one chooses to write them. Or the stories and novels one chooses to read, with author names one cannot now use, are wrenched into a wondrous texture of fiction as turned upon a single wheel. All ate all, while nothing still gnaws at nothing.

THE SHADWELL SHARK

Once upon a time, I often walked into the East End of London from the City where I worked, whether just by extending my lunch break or simply to attend a business meeting nearby which had finished earlier than expected, thus leaving time to kill, or I was simply skiving, I can't now remember. Call it ghost hunting, call it what you will

These streets among which I wandered at random, in the then early 1970s, were not overshadowed by today's monstrously tall vertical sharks as I might call them or as my later verifiable 'synchronised shards of random truth and fiction' called certain other things in that pre-woke era when I used that expression! But soon, in hindsight, I guess I did discern one such shard when walking in Shadwell, or was I actually among other dark wharfsides (where my grandfather once worked), the randomness of my walks often being conflated with my fading memory of them. Limehouse or Wapping, I now have no clue. Well, whichever was the case, I saw a vast black crack in the side of the sky, through which I sensed something eyeing itself through it.

It must have been an occasion, on second thoughts, where I had just left a business meeting with too much of the hard stuff having been circulated. That fact, if fact it were, would explain a lot about what I saw. The streets, even beyond the Square Mile, had buildings with intricate architecture, and

I remember Brick Lane, a thoroughfare that always struck me as if it should have not been a lane at all but a building blocking it throughout from width to length, and, in that vicinity, were certain tops of shop-fronted mansions with messages and codes and carvings near the roofs beyond the normal eye-line of the motley people who happened to be walking the pavements with their heads lowered (they did so then, even without the magnetic power drawing them to consult their smartphones today!).

How this fact of mysteriously arcane tops-to-buildings can be connected with the crack in the sky that I thought I saw as a ghost of itself in the shape of sky high architecture yet to be constructed for real in some distant future, was a question forever overtaken by the sudden wrapping round me of things I could not walk through.

I may be there still. Having found a real ghost but never returnable enough to claim I had found it at last. Not a dream, even if I later woke up at my city desk surrounded by towering piles of files to deal with file by file as work yet to be done that would today be invisible within screens, such duties thus out of sight, out of mind. The sky-eye just lost on some corrupted hard-drive of the future.

THE TALK BIRD

"What is that?" asked one old man called Noel sitting on a sea front bench.

"It's a Talk bird," said the other old man called Leo, sitting with Noel.

"Never heard of it," said Noel, folding and refolding the soft paperback in his lap.

"They used to breed them in the City of London as a means of hearing secrets and then repeating them to the authorities." Leo was an ordinary old man who kept himself alive with eccentric tales to tell, or was completely mad. He was a bit like me. Looked like me, too.

"So why is it here by the sea with the gulls?" asked Noel.

"Just as temporary cover, I guess," said Leo gauchely.

Noel nervously twisted and retwisted the cover of his paperback of ghost stories. And he wondered if words always sounded like they were spelt. Or if anagrams could possibly cancel each other out into nothingness. He then said, wanting to change the subject to something more sensible, "Did you know, Leo, that Clorinda in A.E. Coppard's famous story with that woman's name in the title is an anagram of Ironclad, which is relevant to the plot and essential to understanding it? I think I am the first person to notice that." He, too, was a bit like me.

"Shush!" urged Leo. "The Talk bird has just cocked its ear!"

"Fiddlesticks, that's not called a Talk bird, and if it was, it couldn't do what you say it can do. By the way, there's another story with a secret in this book, a very rare one by Robert Aickman, but I've always liked it. "The Insufficient Answer" it's called, and the answer at outset turns out to be the number 42 and it was written long before Douglas Adams wrote Hitchhiker!"

At that point the Torque bird twirled on its feathered rump into sluggish flight and, like a homing pigeon, clumsily curvetted towards St. Paul's. And Leo and Noel diminished to a tiny mucky residue between the slats of the bench, eventually becoming Nothing, after their partial anagrams as names merged and became a single Drogulus, a word that was once invented by a British philosopher called A.J. Ayer so as to act as the perfect word for the real ghost that the ghost hunter never found. The gulls now screamed in the air.

THE AWKWARD TRANSMISSION OF A TWISTED POSTURE

I knew I had always to think about things in hindsight so as to deduce exactly what had happened, even if the print is fading, and I also needed to reach the end of something to judge the implications of its beginning, give or take the odd intervention by destiny, especially with it being an old eccentric man who stirred such thoughts in me. I had cause to befriend him at the seaside by initially realising that he seemed to be in distress as he tried to walk up from the lower promenade by using the York Road steps instead of his more usual route nearby, he later told me, of the longer but gentler Queensway ZigZag slopes.

"Are you OK?" I asked.

He explained that he had suddenly felt a dizziness, not just in the head but a wrenching of his whole body, a sort of seizure that was not painful but alarming. Despite my parents telling me never to speak to strangers, I took him by the arm and led him eventually from the top of the steps to the nearest bench on the upper promenade. I noted his steep stoop, as he walked.

His immediate words other than the above mention of the ZigZag slopes that he *should* have used, was that he feared he might have changed the whole direction of the world by such an uncharacteristic choice of route back home. I nodded in sympathy with him as I tried to explain the Butterfly Effect or Chaos Theory, but he seemed to know about these phenomena already. He saw that, despite my being much younger than him, I was the sort of person to whom he could talk of similar matters, and he then embarked on a description of a dream he had experienced the previous night, fully expecting me to be patient enough to listen to it.

"I was on the ZigZags at night, Miss, and the sea had a sort of blue darkness, can you imagine that?" He noticed my nod and continued. "And I remembered the pirate radio stations out there with tall masts broadcasting on the Medium Wave with enough reach to stretch as far as London. Anything was better than the dire fading-out and truncations of Radio Luxembourg. Anyway, those ships have long been gone. Listen to the slow swish of the sea. I could actually hear a similar noise within the dream itself, in fact it was the first time I have ever dreamt any sound in any dream. Have you ever dreamt sound, Miss?"

I decided I had never dreamt sound but he continued without waiting for my answer. He described to me a starless and moonless night, yet he could discern what he recognised as the dome of St. Paul's slowly rising from the otherwise placid sea, a vision situated about what he assessed to be a hundred yards from the replenished beach beyond a fishtail groyne. It even more slowly turned on a timely axis, making the sea's surface follow suit. He said it seemed to be a translucent structure, if there had been any light to prove that translucency was possible. Perhaps it had its own light from within, making his own earlier assessment as to its position in the now silent sea thus verified.

It then faded beyond potential light with a silence more silent than silence itself. Or did it sink as slowly as it rose. The dream was foreshortened, and I cannot remember any more. I hope I didn't miss anything out.

TUGGED HIS FINGERS FREE

I was in evident burn-out, my stories becoming more and more truncated. What should I do but quickly write another story, even if dangerously tailgating the previous one. Prove them wrong, old son, I say to myself. Be direct, shed any co-narrator, and be freehold not leasehold in what you already own the ownership of narrating.

Yet, just as that urging had been said, I sensed another presence in the room, the ghost we hunt made manifest. Ah, just then, in the previous sentence, you somehow slid into the first person plural.

You need to stick with the singular person you are, always have been and always will be, and then firmly persist with it. But your pronoun has morphed yet again, even before you realised you had by now slipped into the second person as a corruption of the first. Only the shadowy third can surely follow.

Pronouns were now coming out of the walls as packs of squirming worms, the biting points of their screws compromising the very integrity of the bungalow house where he had chosen to live for many years. His body was a shadow of itself, his mind straddling the vast distance between who he used to be and who he will now become. They ate his eyes, feasted upon his soul, tugged his fingers free, and used his own words for telling this, as if these words were their own words instead. Words that told me I had to attend some court of judgment to hear my sentence said.

A MAELSTROM OF MINIATURES

When I first started the earlier Miniatures with Mansions a few weeks ago, I little believed we would end up here with different miniatures, different turnings. As well as being a ghost hunter acting as a ghost establisher I later started being employed as ghost exorcist proper. Burn-out on some arched motorway or heavenly bridge. Now a reteller or reviser or purger of memories and words without names, but certainly with lots of wiggle room and play. An exorcist not in any sense of cruelty to ghosts nor as a simple helper of human beings to rid themselves of fears, but mainly to ease ghosts into a proper death whereby their own fears can be added to the nothingness they had so far dodged. There was a man, for example, who had a large amount of statuary in his bungalow's front garden near where I lived at the seaside but, when invited inside to do my business, I found quite a large detailed model of St Paul's Cathedral on his sitting-room floor with a handle, as if it were a fruit machine or an old-fashioned clattering calculator with which I had once worked near the National Gallery in London, something you may recall from earlier. He wanted me to turn that handle for the first time and, with a wrench, I duly did, and so the stories flowed like a fruit machine jackpot…..

***

The man had been stationed in the Gallery and, as if he were one of the wardens who usually sit in the corner of each room to guard the paintings, he now watched the desultory groups of art-goers as they came and went. It was a Show loosely depicting clowns and circuses through the ages. An exhibition perhaps more suitable for an East End gallery nearer St Paul's itself than Pall Mall.

He had been hired for the day complete with his clown outfit to wander from room to room – thus to grant some Big Top atmosphere to proceedings. However, he was tired and had filched a warden's chair so as to give his legs a rest. Toulouse-Lautrec (I am now allowed to cite dead names if not living ones in this series of tales) faced him and he studied the original painting as if it were the painter himself. He held imaginary conversations with him – only rarely interrupted by a new supply of art-goers in ones and twos who wandered through having wondered why he was tucked away in this room instead of greeting people at the main door. His baggy white tunic's black rosettes and even his red nose sunk back into the shadows.

But then came three visitors who stayed longer than welcome – at least from our man's point of view. These visitors evidently didn't know each other, having arrived in this part of the Gallery by chance. They stared singly at each painting, returning time and time again to one particular painting which we couldn't see, along with our man, from where he was sitting in the gloom. He hadn't bothered to inspect each painting in the room before deciding to plump down in the fortuitously vacant chair. He had not even wondered to where the room's warden had vanished. They were supposed to relieve each other. He didn't get on with the wardens. They probably thought that his own role was a waste of time. A mere gimmick, bringing the show into tacky disgrace.

He turned his attention to the three visiting art-sticklers in the room. He took unconscious pride in fathoming people by just looking at them. Indeed, unknown to himself, he had a tiny creature inside – separate from his brain but seeing through his eyes. This creature could dig deeper and more seriously into reality than the outward slapstick of his job as a clown could ever otherwise promise to deliver.

One of the visitors was a Civil Servant, lover of Oscar Wilde's wit, obsessed with tidiness, lover of Amateur Dramatics – who said "Mmm, Nice" as he approached each painting. The second was a middle-aged woman, unemployed, with a West Country accent even before she spoke aloud … but she did say something eventually with a "I'm sooooo tired!" to herself. The third was another woman, age 27, Administrator at a 6th Form College, someone who complained a lot, cynical about love or romance, and said, for no apparent reason, into the empty air: "I have never been drunk." She had, by saying this, merely spoken aloud the title on one of the labels next to a painting depicting a clown who was apparently the only sober person centrally among many ordinarily dressed people who were riotously drunk. The clown, acting clownishly, also appeared drunk, but was acting the part of being drunk. One would need a lot of empathy to gather exactly the moral of the painting or its wider interpretation. For example, was the clown drunk, and were the others acting drunk?

Taken up by these hidden considerations, our protagonist man and even his inner creature had forgotten to continue fathoming the characters of the three visitors to the room, visitors who now seemed to have pitched their metaphorical tents for the duration, not one of them yet, however, communicating with the others, let alone with our man himself. They did gradually and more consistently gravitate towards one particular painting that we could now see in our mind's eye even if our man, as our viewpoint, could not see it for real from where he sat. He pictured a portrait of himself sitting in the corner of the room. A poignant image of a sad clown or jester. But why did the three visitors not therefore visibly compare the painting to his presence in the corner? Surely they had spotted the resemblance and marvelled at the coincidence. He felt their gaze penetrate his baggy costume even as far as the distinguishing marks of his sunken chest and strawberry birthmark on his back. It was as if the painting was him and he was otherwise nowhere to be seen. He was urged to get up and start clowning about. Unlike most clowns, he could perform alone, so it would not be difficult to ad lib within the rarefied space he inhabited. After all, that was what he was being paid for – to give an atmosphere of the circus and its clowns.

But why should he? These were chance, unconnected visitors, each with their own agenda, each with their separate paths to the Gallery and, later, away from it. He could tell at least that fact from their very chance names we have not been able to divulge, their chance jobs, and their chance ill-chosen words. Let them make what they could of the unmakeable. Of the unremarkable.

He'd give them no pleasure of synchronicity or serendipity. That wasn't his job. He was there merely as a clown in a vacuum jar. Or just another frozen exhibit on the wall. But it was wishful thinking to imagine that he had no role to play other than simply to be just there.

He saw sinewy tendrils winding slowly in the air between the three visitors, a communication system of which they were evidently unaware. But which of them would break the silence first and to whom and why? The question remained in the air as they finally struck camp and left the Gallery, almost together, for the outside world.

The chair's warden now returned to the room and gave our man a piece of his mind – to get going, circulate, make a brouhaha of welcome, get out on the street, rustle up a few more viewers for the Gallery… A clown among disguised clowns.

Not to be rushed, our man sluggishly left the chair to its rightful owner and, before finally leaving the room, he walked over to discover half-heartedly what painting the three visitors had earlier gravitated towards. It was a meticulously detailed painting of St Paul's Cathedral, recognisable as such while straddling something more than simply squatting upon it, and, beside it, even conjoined to it, was an in-scale version of Nelson's column slowly, he guessed, tilting downward.

NAAN BREAD AND SLIPPERS

Shopping lists tend to be eclectic as well as quite lengthy. However, the day I visited Colchester to see my elderly Mother, her list was much shorter than normal, but equally eclectic. We needed to pass back, after shopping, through the St Botolph's Priory Ruins as a short cut to where she lived a sheltered life.

But the rest of that trip must remain a private one – now completed, but in addition to what my mother had purchased, I obtained a peshwari naan bread and new carpet slippers fitting my feet and later worn about the house.

So, we'll leave my shopping list of two items to become another fiction of history, just a non-event eventually to become a false memory of something real. This is as much of life (now, then or forever) that one can manage.

Time itself, if not eclectic, *is* very lengthy. But one simply allows it to slip by without the consciousness of recalled choice: too easily oiled by non-stick serendipity or fast-fading existence.

Sadly, my story is therefore about a man whose need for naan bread and slippers was as fictitious as the need to be *himself*. A nothing dreamed by a nothingness.

His beloved mother became a dead silent ghost by his side,

even if, at best, her walking-stick could still be heard clicking along Colchester's pavements. The comforting familiarity of her shrill voice echoing from the past … or *pre*-echoing a time when she, as another ghost, shadowed an earlier self that was even less real than she would become. Shadowy Thirds all of them at different stages.

The man's responses were slightly out of rhythm with the real man he surely must once have been – out of rhythm but synchronised *enough* to foster a feasible belief in himself.

The slippers were too soft to make sound in the comfort zones of Heaven. But I was now *less* than nothing – not even a fictitious ghost. Only a tattered shopping-list slipping away in a very tiny tornado. And Naan became a new mystical word for Nothingness.

THE CUPOLA

They ended up not *wanting* to have names. A group of people who ripped off their unseen labels one by one. There needed to be an example set, however. Nobody would un-name themselves without a lead to follow. A First Mover. The pre-emptive Clockmaker. If this were a proper story, the author would start with the example-setting character's name – followed by a narrative of his rite-of-passage from name to namelessness. A tale of bravery and hardship, of a dimmer-switch controlling the light of the character's identity, of those who failed to follow and remained named, of those who did follow and *became* unnamed.

Yet to name the leading character as he was once named would be to jam the dimmer-switch by wedging in what the character itself was trying to dim. The others who remained named would gain prominence by having real characters' names in the story while the rest floundered about unidentified – not only confusing the pecking-orders within the plot but the plot itself. To call them by false names or even by letters like A, B, C would, no doubt, cloud the issue even further. Meanwhile, it's good for any story's author to relax and concentrate on the plot's landscape, its spirit of place, before worrying about the entrance of characters,

The public park in Colchester, with Norman Castle, flowerneatened gardens, an empty bandstand the tiny original of which decorates, as a cupola, the top of the nearby Wivenhoe church tower. In the park, meantime, the castle and its gardens eventually led down grassy slopes, somehow circularly zigzagging, towards a small boating-lake in the park's valley. Nobody has hired a boat today. It must be one of those times when everyone is asleep at home. The Longest Day of the year. Light at Night like the Land of the Midnight Sun. Or the irrecurrent Blue Moon. Even here in England's Essex. With the dimmer-switch of the Sun turned right up.

Without people, there can be no story to tell. But now, at first dimly seen, are tall dark shadows wandering around the Castle. They are the nameless Masters of Existence trying to form gradually into real people. They have been given no belief in the story-premise that all the real people are at home sleeping. Yet the Masters, so-called, remain only partly formed into what they had hoped to become since the story had given them no names other than as fictionalised Masters of Existence, no names on which to hang their identities. The story refused them any such luxury. So mere shadows (if slightly flesh-corrupted) they have remained, still circling the Castle like forgotten druids. Masters of Existence who could not even master existence for themselves!

Suddenly, there appeared, on the margins of the boating-lake, the legendary Clockmaker whose clocks had hands but no numbers but, sometimes, numbers but no hands, because, with the former, one could at least guess the time they told. A real flesh-and-blood person, this Clockmaker.

As taught by Masters, but lacking their ambition of existence, the Clockmaker actually succeeded in becoming what they had desired but failed to be. The Clockmaker knew that any ambition destroys the goal of that same ambition.

And now is time for waking. We are here, stretching and yawning, fully-formed, still nameless, as stirred by many pre-alarmed timepieces within our minds, but we are pure of heart and unconstrained by the deadlines of finding identities to wrap ourselves in. Owning identities simply by yearning for identities to own, because the only pre-condition for having an identity is not to have one at all.

And the story can at last begin. From the boating lake, there slowly rose the tip of a huge turning cathedral dome with its own cupola as the timepiece's essential gnomon.

DROWSY WITH DIVINITY

There was an exhibition of paintings of women with their backs to us. I, as a woman, wondered why anyone would think to paint these paintings or arrange such a display of mixed motives: scornful watchfuless, loving care at a distance, stalking, pining…

In fact, these name-hidden presences hung on gallery walls have given me some of the clues as to the possible permutations of reaction to such a 'happening' of themed images.

As I walked around the gallery, I tried to put myself in the mind of each man who stood or sat behind each woman in the paintings … thus concocting for myself a new recipe of tempting emotions fitting for such an apparently bleak, often oblique experience.

Have you ever sensed eyes boring into your back? You dare not turn for whatever reason. It's almost as if you are guilty about catching someone looking at you surreptitiously. They're to blame for their own actions (or inaction in not looking away) but *you* feel guilty that you may have stirred their curiosity, their longing, distaste or even gratuitousness of idle gaze.

Well, today, that day, whenever it was to be, in that gallery-of-few-visitors but many guards-sitting-in-corners, you now somehow gazed at the backviews of each painting itself, knowing, in some intrinsic dream bordering on nightmare, that you were staring outward from the frame you could no longer see …. and you cried inwardly as you felt itches crawling along your back and nape of neck between canvas and frame's backing. Or between canvas and paint. You could not be sure. Just the distant echo of a shout from a corner-guard whose words were deadened by the glass.

Later, I was filled by some greater sense of existence, ironically a drowsiness with divinity in various roles of painterly art. To the distant sound of violins, drums and flutes, reminding us that the planet's paintings are subject to the twists of precarious immortality just as our own mortality is assured.

THE HAUNTED MANSION

They lived here for real, many centuries ago. Today, they are ghosts. Right now, under my nose. Or, rather, if the truth be known, they live for real today — and many centuries ago their ghosts lived here first. Real people as the eventual fulfilment-in-flesh of their earlier ghosts. In many ways, that seems to be the most logical order of things. For centuries, people have believed we precede our ghosts, while all along ghosts preceded us.

But that begs a question – where is *here?* It is Haunted Mansion on the road between Colchester and Chelmsford – once well known for receiving visitors on day trips, but, today, a near-forgotten hulk where the old family – now on hard times – manages to cling on. I am their only member of staff: a man-with-many-tricks-of-the-trade, they call me. A do-it-all who haunts the Mansion in a real body, mending broken things and, if the truth be known, breaking things so that I can mend them again. Indeed, I do jobs not only for the old family but also for the even older family – trying to match up the old with the less old when and where they happen to coincide in the same part of the Mansion. That's what I call make-do and mend. Helping people meet their own ghosts – across time.

You may wonder whether I have managed to coincide with myself across the centuries in the Mansion that haunts the older version of itself and me. Except when it was older, it was, of course, newer. Which goes for us all, I guess. And tonight is the night when I shall mend myself and my guilt. I shall discover the broken body with the knife I placed into its chest so very long ago. The knife still sticking out of it like a handle. And then I shall slowly, ever so slowly try not to hurt him, while watching the smile return to his mouth before I can even realise he is *trying* to smile – trying to smile at *me*. And as he does so, I feel tears arrive in my eyes. Noise of the traffic outside on the A12 highway hiding the sound of what I did next. Just a careful twist and turn like a surgeon, then nothing.

The way at last to begin hunting *the* ghost is by actually finding it first?

OLD LID

Today, with the lamplighter having been called out early as a duty to counter fog, it didn't seem to matter how old the two self-portraits I found in an attic happened to be, as they were obviously older than anyone alive today, but just which of the two men (or who appeared to be two men) owned them last of all and had thus been responsible for leaving this evidence of their life together in two mutually painted portraits in separate configurations of a shared would-be joy? Whatever the answer, I assumed these paintings, separated by frames, had been completed with oils from the same tubes and mixed upon the same palette, using the same palette knife that helped thickly smear the ready-made craquelure over the youthfulness and hope beneath it. Whether the two subjects, as sitters for themselves if not for each other, needed to disguise their fresh respective likenesses in this way, they certainly had been left with a twisted torment facing up front. I delved into the backs behind the canvases to find what markings I could below the painted surfaces that were, in turn, behind the vertical glass lids, as I painstakingly unnailed such backs, the dusty wood-bases of the equally vertical containers to allow the parallel transparent lids to stay in place above the faces. The final shocking realisation was that, despite two backs, it possessed only one framed frontage effectively holding a single slow-blinking eyelid, with notably tickly lashes uncurling after being laced, until their new freedom today, within the texture of paint, the eye itself seeming to be like a slug with a pupil, still alive however many centuries had since gone by. Not a diptych, as such, to have its backs scratched, but something else altogether previously unknown to the art world, soon to become a new movement in Aesthetics and a philosophical watershed. A canny arrangement of bodily assuagement with oodles of abraded grey later discovered to be under the front counter of colour. Whether perpetrated by master or student, or by both, the result, now newly gaslit as a whole, was priceless. Indeed, it was the Real Mucky. A joy fulfilled.

A Tribute to D.F. Lewis (Des to His Friends)

By David Mathew

1

It was only after I had accepted the invitation to write this Introduction that it occurred to me to ask myself: "Which Des? Which Des shall I introduce?"

Des the Author? This would seem logical, in an Introduction to a new volume of the man's shorter fiction. His published pieces number well into the thousands, so Des the Prolific Author, perhaps? Des the Ghost Story Author? Des the Miniaturist Author? The last is equally valid, I would argue, in the sense that many of his characters leave their marks on the page in hundreds, rather than thousands, of words. All of these des-criptive subdivisions are true of the wonderful volume that these words intend to introduce.

But where would that leave Des the Editor, the mind behind The Horror Anthology of Horror Anthologies (among others)? An anthology of short stories, each of which had to reference another horror anthology! (I chose Alfred Hitchcock's Ghostly Gallery. I was proud to have been selected for inclusion in what became known as The HA of HA, a very Des title…) Or Des the Editor of Nemonymous, the fiction magazine into whose whiter-than-white landscape pages it was a privilege and a rite of passage to be accepted? Where would that leave Des the Real-Time Reviewer, who created his unique, brilliant, witty and iterative reviews through the course of reading the book or short story in question, rather than as a summative statement at the end of a reading? Or Des the A.I. Enthusiast? Des the Photographer? Or Des the Friend? In short, which of his many (and multi-coloured) hats is Des (or D.F.) Lewis wearing at the moment?

Let us state the obvious. Des Lewis is not the same man (not exactly or not at all?) as D.F. Lewis, but nor would we expect him to be. A pen name is launched for a reason, and D.F. Lewis has been a pen name for decades. (Once upon a time, I asked Des what his day-job colleagues thought of his inspiring, prodigious publishing career. "They don't know anything about it," was the reply.) However, Des Lewis and D.F. Lewis are not two separate, discrete men either. Both evolving, iterative drafts of this artist are quiddities; each contains multitudes; and I do not know which of them I know the best – although, if pushed, I would probably plump for Des (at this very moment… but we know how fickle the simple art of interpretation can become: Des has taught us this much, as well).

When Mike Sauve asked if I would like to write this Introduction, I started to think about how our writing lives have not so much run in parallel as overlapped at certain important points. Think of waves on a beach, advancing and withdrawing, with irregular pulls and pools, and with spumes inter-slurping. Or why not make the matter more specific? Make it Clacton beach, for this is Des we are des-cussing, and as most people reading these words will be aware, Des has lived in the Clacton area of England for decades. Quite often he entertains us with a photograph from a wander along the seafront. He always finds something interesting to show us; and for me, personally, he has done so from the beginning of my own writing life. Please allow me a moment to explain this comment.

2

For a while, at the end of the millennium and in the early days of a new century, Des and I (and others who formed part of a writers and artists collective called Storyville), became entranced by the concept – and even the word – serendipity. The word was in the air, in the waves; it was everywhere… for a while. Things happen by such random chance (it was proposed) that one cannot believe there was not a design in there somewhere, even if one has to step miles back to see the mechanisms, the patterns and the personnel. Was it good fortune or was it design that drew Des and me into one another's orbits? Well, like attracts like, I suppose, but there was more. There was Storyville, of course (on the subject of which more will follow); and I believe that it was during the early months of Storyville that I became aware of an example of (why not? – one more time, for luck) serendipity.

My first professional sale was a short story called "New Arrivals, Old Escapes"; it was published in a small press magazine called New Visions in 1989. The hour or two that I had spent writing it, in a no-longer-there café in what was then the Arndale Centre, Luton, had seemed an excellent time investment. On publication, I earned myself £3 – and I hadn't even left the Sixth Form to go to university! I was made! ("The HA of HA" might also be a way of des-scribing sarcastic laughter; but that is another story.)

A mere thirty-five years later (what's a decade?), and I found myself reflecting on that first sale. Shall we praise the Internet at this point? To my astonishment, the magazine New Visions is listed on the Internet Speculative Fiction

Database. The reason that I mention this is because I shared the Contents Page with one D.F. Lewis, who had submitted a story with the very Des-like title of "The Laying Down of Haze". And how I only wish that I still had the magazine, but here are the details, as large as life.

It would be some further years before I learned of Lewis's prodigious fictional output; perhaps it was our shared time in Storyville that was my teacher. Certainly, 'The Laying Down of Haze is but one story in the thousands that D.F. Lewis has published… and as you can see from The Ghost-hunter, the book in your hand or on the screen in front of you, he is still going strong, very strong; still adding to that formidable, frightening tally. While I went off to Bangor University, Des went on his lunch break from the day job and pumped out a few hundred words – I believe in long-hand, in a notebook – most days of the working week. It need not matter that his day-job colleagues had no idea of what he was doing while he ate his sandwiches. Other colleagues and other friends (other voices in other rooms) knew exactly of the changes that Des had brought, and would continue to bring, to Weird Fiction. Indeed, we will hear from some of them in this Introduction: collegiality and friendship are important components of the artist's life, and no less so for Lewis than for anyone else.

To return to my original questions: "Which Des? Which Des shall I introduce?" – we might start with those warm and fruitful days in the Storyville collective already mentioned. I invited contributions from members of that group and from colleagues and friends from further afield, as long as they had a connection to Des (or D.F.) Lewis. And while I should add that at this point of writing (early September

2024) Des does not know that I am writing his Introduction, the people who responded to my invitation surely do. My gratitude – to the contributors, and of course to Des – soars wide on wings of song.

3

Shall we start with the fiction? The fiction is what I imagine we are here for, predominantly – even if Des's fiction has always lived and breathed alongside his other artistic endeavours. For instance, Liz Williams tells us: "When I first met Des online on Storyville, I was stunned by the sheer force and uniqueness of his imagination. A work of his fiction is always an event." But what was Storyville? It has been mentioned several times up to now. To explain Storyville to anyone who was not there and then, here are the words of Iain Rowan:

> What was Storyville? A loose collective of writers spread over the UK and the US, usually with broadly common tastes in weird fiction. It was like an online writing group, working through email, that was both a social thing but also allowed space for critique and advice. It felt like an extended, supportive family of writers. It was already well underway by the time that I found it. As a new writer, I found somewhere that felt like home: supportive, encouraging, playful, helpful. I loved being able to celebrate in the successes of others, and over the time of its existence saw some wonderful moves forward for members. It

was small enough to feel sociable, but not so tiny it was an echo chamber, and the support and encouragement I got shaped me as a writer.

Perhaps my favourite memory is one of the two times I managed to get to a meet up. This one was in a fabulous and inspiring place – in Robin Hood's Bay – in an incredible venue – an old manor house we rented. Sitting in the main room of the manor, late at night, a fair few glasses of wine in, listening to everyone read what they had been working on was, and will remain, one of the best moments writing has ever brought me.

It was through Storyville that I got to know Keith Brooke, who ended up publishing me for Infinity Plus, and Des Lewis, which is why I submitted to and was published in Nemonymous, and Jeff Vandermeer, which is how a couple of pieces of mine ended up in the hugely entertaining Thackery T Lambshead Pocket Guide to Eccentric and Discredited Diseases.

Lovely as it was, I do think that sometimes things have a natural lifecycle, and it's maybe better to let them go with grace than hang on. But Storyville was one of the best social networks of any kind, and I look back on it, and all involved with it, with lots of fond memories and not a single bad one.

Iain continues:

> D.F. Lewis. Des. Or perhaps simply the author, editor, reviewer, thinker and all-round good person who shall remain nemonymous. I had the privilege of meeting Des on the writers' group Storyville, many, many years ago. I was very much the new kid on the block, with no experience, but Des and the others in that wonderful group encouraged, coached, shared. It was down to Des that my first published short story saw the light of day. "Ice Age" appeared in the second edition of Nemonymous, a typical D.F. Lewis venture of "parthenogenic fiction and late labelling". Stories appeared in the journal anonymously, and the authors were only revealed in the next issue when it came out. Apart from it being stacked with great stories by some terrific authors chosen by Des with his eye for the weird and wonderful, it was a beautiful, mysterious object that ran for nine years. Des kept encouraging, kept supporting, ever generous with his time, even though there were so many demands upon him from his own prolific writing, his editing, his publishing, his real-time reviewing that's been on the go for nearly two decades.
>
> One last fond memory: many of the Storyville crew met up on his home turf of Walton-on-Naze and Clacton, went wandering, kept talking, Des the weirdmonger our guide and guru. As then, as so many other times.

None of the people who wrote in response to my invitation knows what anyone else contributed, but I encourage the reader to consider links, thematic or otherwise. As Keith has been mentioned by Iain, let us go to Keith Brooke next. Keith?

> Des? A lovely, gentle soul, who always came across as very quiet, but you soon realised there was a lot more going on in his souped-up brain.
>
> My favourite recollections, apart from the Storyville jolly in Robin Hood's Bay, are from a short period when I used to meet up with him and Lawrence Dyer for our north Essex walks. We'd pick a different location each time – Mistley Towers, Jaywick, Mersea Island and more – and somehow would always end up in a pub after our walk.
>
> Over a pint and some food, we would talk about what we'd seen and that would start sparking story ideas. Then, after our farewells, and usually on the same day, one of us would write the opening to a story and send it to the other two. Then someone else would pick it up and add some more, and we'd pass the story around between the three of us until we had a magically weird tale that none of us could have written alone.
>
> Somehow that strange process worked, and all three stories we produced this way found a home. And if you write out the titles in order of writing ("Fruit of the Flotsam", "Wooden Boys Don't Bleed", "Visitors"), you kind of get a micro-story

> in its own right, or at least the title of one: Fruit of the flotsam, wooden boys don't bleed visitors.

We will come back to the idea of collaborative writing shortly, but for now, as Lawrence has been mentioned ("Tag!"), let us go next to Lawrence Dyer, to tells us:

> Des takes an intuitive or instinctual approach in his work, seeking out aspects of perception and existence hidden to or ignored by others. The result is a rich tapestry of perceptions and feelings that provide his unique vision. They are the kind of things that might serve as background were they to appear in the writings of the less perceptive, but through his particular approach Des elevates them to the foreground and explores them in depth in their own right, so creating his distinctive approach to literature.

Rosanne Rabinowitz picks up the thread, referencing The Third Alternative magazine when she mentions TTA.

> I met Des through a TTAPress email chat group in the latter 1990s. We later met in person at informal TTA mini-cons held in London and Cambridge. I also have fond memories of a walk around Clacton with a group of friends. We ended up at his place to watch Koyaanisqatsi and enjoy food, drink and lively discussion of the film and everything else.
>
> Des was always an enthusiastic supporter of my

> work and I'm proud that he selected my stories for two of his anthologies – Horror Without Victims and The Horror Anthology of Horror Anthologies. I am always in awe of his real-time reviews and appreciated his commentary on my stories and my book, Resonance & Revolt. An insightful review will prod a writer to look at their work in a new way, and Des's fabulous stream of thought and reflections have done that for me.
>
> (BTW Des, I do have plans to put "The Pearl and the Boil" in a future collection!)

Before we move to the real-time reviews, let us stay with Koyaanisqatsi for a moment. Tamar Yellin has an anecdote that echoes Rosanne's memories. Tamar writes:

> My first encounter with Des Lewis, when I joined the Storyville online writers' group in 1999, was as the legendary figure D. F. Lewis – legendary for both the numinous and prolific nature of his work. Storyville was a wonderfully lively and effervescent community, of which Des was unquestionably the paterfamilias. For a few years it was a crucible to many creative minds. I discovered D. F. Lewis's short fiction chiefly through the Weirdmonger collection that appeared from Prime in 2003. Nobody writes quite like him. One of the story openings that still sticks in my mind is the cry of the night soil man: «Cheap turds! Cheap turds!» His fiction is weird, outrageous, terrifying and poignant by turns, and always unpredictable.
>
> Towards the end of the Storyville period Des es-

> tablished Nemonymous magazine, to which writers contributed anonymously. It was a typically generous and original venture of his. His great generosity towards other writers is a part of his legend: his real-time reviews being only its latest iteration. He certainly gave me encouragement at a time when it was most needed and has continued to champion my work. Once the Storyville gang visited Des at his home in Clacton. He and his wife Denise entertained us sumptuously, finishing up with a showing of Koyaanisqatsi in their front room. We sat there mesmerised. Des turned to Denise. "I've hypnotised the children," he said.

The real-time reviews have been important to so many of us. Julie Travis writes:

> Des's fiction reviews have long been the stuff of legend. They're written in real time; that is, he writes/posts as he reads, the result being an in-depth review that's a work of art in its own right. He's reviewed many of my stories over the years and I've always seen it as an honour.
>
> I met Des some thirty years ago at an informal writers' meet-up in a pub near London's Victoria station. At the time I'd only had a couple of stories published, whereas he was well known and writing a short story every day. He was a gent, very approachable, and we had plenty to talk about.
>
> I disappeared from the UK "slipstream" fiction

> scene after that, for well over a decade. On my return he was very welcoming and remembered our meeting all those years before.

Andrew Hook is also complimentary about the real-time reviews:

> Des Lewis's Real-Time Reviews often drew dots to show connections that I wasn't aware existed. I always felt Des really 'got' my work in ways that others didn't. That kind of in depth, on-the-go review was eagerly anticipated and the benefit to any writer was enormous. Combine that with his own prolific fiction output and you have a national treasure!

And Jetse de Vries would like to say a few additional words in praise of Nemonymous.

> Back in the early 2000s I flew over to the UK to attend several of the informal TTAPress meet-ups and was privileged to meet a number of legendary people from the British Small Press, in particular Andy Cox (yes, he does exist) and Des Lewis.
>
> In those days, Des was doing a Nemonymous edition every year, and in the first five editions Andy Cox was the designer and typesetter, meaning two legends working together. The stories were submitted and published anonymously, and it was an open secret that every writer—and I do mean every single one, don't lie—from the British Small Press (and many beyond) wanted to be published

in Nemonymous.

Des scrupulously read all the anonymous submissions and published what he thought worked best for the Nemonymous concept. Des is a kind soul and an incredibly prolific writer, yet I was chuffed immensely when he accepted a story of mine for Nemonymous 4. And I fondly remember basking in the glow of fame being able to say I was published in Nemonymous after issue 5 was released at a TTAPress meeting, sharing this with several other attendees while I could see in the eyes of at least one of them (hello Paul Meloy…;-) that they weren't allowed to announce it quite yet, but that they were just as chuffed as me.

Thanks, Des, for bringing this beauty to our lives!

4

Those Storyville days were fecund with collaborations. In terms of creativity and output, we worked together and found other voices in other rooms. The air bristled with energy, and it seems now that no sooner was one collaboration finished than another began. We could scarcely control ourselves! Literarily speaking, some of us swung like billy-o. Des and I collaborated on a handful of tales, sometimes along with third and even fourth parties. For example, a volume called Die Earthman Die: Tales of Horror and SF boasts four names on the cover – M.F. Korn, D.F. Lewis, Mike Philbin and David Mathew – and the stories within are co-authored by every combination of our names. At the back of the book, in the author biographies, D.F. Lewis has written: “The original DFL was born in 1948 only a few miles from where he lives now…” I love that original.

I remember being excited to collaborate. Despite my early publishing start while still a schoolboy, I had published some shorter fiction but not lots. Storyville members seemed productive and knowledgeable; they appeared to know what to do. At the time I had spent much of my writing energy on non-fiction, journalism and reviewing. With one of my collaborations with Des, I think I had written half a page or a page, and I passed it over with my ideas and notes for how he might consider continuing. Des wrote back quickly, with my notes and ideas copied into the body of the email, and a single sentence of his own: “I can’t do anything with this.” He would not be able to plot using someone else’s forward thinking: that’s not who he was as an author. Although I would not say that planning was anathema to him (I honestly don’t know this one way or the other, although the restless nature of real-time reviewing gives some credence to the notion), I would venture that he slipped into a groove when he wrote – and I believe when he writes, up to this day.

Reminiscences aside, and tributes (I hope) having landed well, without too many splashes where the rock pools intersect, we have a book to prepare ourselves for. The Ghosthunter is a fresh look at the modern world, using the traditional plot devices of hauntings and hunting. While recognising the spillages of ghosts into our contemporary milieux, we gratefully acknowledge many a flick of a well-timed phrase. For example, the following is by D.F. Lewis, from “As Texted Late One Night to a Random Recipient” (a title soaked in the spirit of Laurie Lee). This is what you are getting in this book, and the price of admission does not necessarily permit the reader to exit. No matter; we are all going to get our emotional money’s worth.

> I top the hill with my hiking boots just as the sun is setting and discern two mansions and two churches close to some afforestation that appear to be unmapped by Google but self-evidently (because I had started off that morning hiking there!) within the precincts of Suffolk, not far from Rendlesham. You see, I usually enjoyed not knowing where I was going and where I was due to stay the night and did not even carry a tent because I simply knew serendipity and weather were usually my friends amidst such voluntary directionlessness — unless I was forced to break such a rule when becoming out so late, darkness being its own weather, and still without a roof to cover me.
>
> Neither of the mansions appear to be hotels; the churches, too close to each other for comfort, are obviously last resorts even when given the kindness of a friendly priest, curate, verger or sexton. I have no illusions. This was no longer the era of Walter de la Mare, and I now admit I was often disappointed by my own serendipity at the end of the day.

I would like to close with a few more words about friendship – and meaningful ties.

In a spirit of homage, I gave the name Des Lewis to a rival wrong-'un character in a series of related short stories that fed into my novel Dreadnought Flex. (Dreadnought and Des had been enemies for longer than either of them had imagined, and not only in West London either.) Des found my deployment of his name for a gangster character amusing. Furthermore, the fact that I dedicated my novel Abandoned Dental Clinics to Des should probably confirm my appreciation of all that he has done for me. I wrote:

Dedicated to Des Lewis.
Not the villain in some of my fictions,
but the real Des Lewis.
A gentleman, a scholar and an acrobat,
if ever I knew one.
"Uncle Des."
Thank you.

The draft of Des that I have been proud to know and call a friend is a character in a pub scene, or on a beach walk, or at a convention hosted by the British Fantasy Society. Nursing pints of bitter (I think Des drinks bitter – the fact that I cannot remember speaks of too many years having passed without rendezvous), we would talk books and music, occasionally politics; sometimes just the two of us, sometimes with a rotating crew of other party members, including our much-loved and much-missed mutual friend Joel Lane, who passed away unexpectedly in 2013, at the age of fifty, and who I am sure Des will not mind me mentioning in an Introduction dedicated to his new book.

There is (of course!) another reason for mentioning Joel at this point. A D.F. Lewis-like moment arrived the morning after I had sat in my garden and written on the post-it notes that structured my thinking for this Introduction. I sat down to read the entry on LEWIS, D(Esmond) Francis in the St James Guide to Horror, Ghost and Gothic Writers, utterly convinced – positive – that the entry had been written by Mike Ashley, all those years ago. I was wrong. The entry was authored by Joel Lane. Joel had managed to find his way back into my life, and into Des's life, bless him, even when I least expected his spirit to arrive. He also used the word restless in his excellent piece; and as he has been so good as to raise a smile, let us leave the last words to Joel Lane, from the final paragraph of what he had to say about Des Lewis in that reference guide.

> The overall development of D.F. Lewis's work over the decade has been towards greater length and continuity: from the stinging, angry brevity of the early work towards a more discursive, structured approach which recalls the metaphysical ghost stories of Robert Aickman. Lewis's work is as remarkable for its intensity, poetic flair and bitter passion as for its protean scope and variety… his status is unassailable – both as a figurehead of horror fiction's avant-garde and as a dedicated excavator of its traditions.

References

Pringle, D. (Ed.) (1998). St James Guide to Horror, Ghost & Gothic Writers. London: St James Press.

BIO

THE THREE AGES of D.F. LEWIS (1948 -)

1. Weirdmonger: (1986 - 1999): A thousand published stories.

2. Nemonymous et al (2001 - 2013): Publisher of other writers.

3. Gestalt (2008 to date): groundbreaking Real-Time Reviews of other writers' fiction. Plus one novel together with some book collections and novellas published independently. And visual image and photo making on a large amateur scale.

Printed in Dunstable, United Kingdom

70878456R00078